"It *Is* Your Signature, Ms. Ford," He Said. "And Now You Owe Me Two Hundred Thousand Dollars."

Her head snapped up, her eyes wide and panicked. "But I don't have that kind of money."

God she was beautiful.

His gaze slid down her simple pink dress and matching jacket, to the slender legs revealed by the hem of her dress.

They'd look really sexy in a tub filled with bubbles, one shapely calf raised as she smoothed soap over its silky length, the water's edge just stopping short of covering her breasts. The image aroused him without any effort at all, sending the blood pounding through his veins, telling him he needed a woman.

This woman.

Dear Reader,

This is my second book for Silhouette Desire and I'm just as excited and thrilled about it as my first one. Writing for the Desire line is such a dream come true for me.

And just like my first book, this one is also set in Darwin in the tropical north of Australia, where I lived for many years with my family. It's a special setting that deserves a unique story for my characters. I loved writing about a rich, arrogant hero who falls for a beautiful woman pregnant with another man's child. It takes a special couple to make something like that work. Of course, all those balmy sun-filled days and long summer nights might have helped Flynn and Danielle fall in love just a little.

I hope you enjoy this book and that you will look forward to reading my next book due for release in August 2007. Damien's story is the third book in the AUSTRALIAN MILLIONAIRES series.

Happy reading!

Maxine

MAXINE SULLIVAN

THE TYCOON'S BLACKMAILED MISTRESS

Published by Silhouette Books

America's Publisher of Contemporary Romance

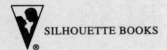

SILHOUETTE BOOKS

ISBN-13: 978-0-373-76800-4
ISBN-10:   0-373-76800-1

THE TYCOON'S BLACKMAILED MISTRESS

Visit Silhouette Books at www.eHarlequin.com

Printed in U.S.A.

Books by Maxine Sullivan

Silhouette Desire

The Millionaire's Seductive Revenge #1782
The Tycoon's Blackmailed Mistress #1800

*Australian Millionaires

MAXINE SULLIVAN

credits her mother for her lifelong love of romance novels, so it was a natural extension to want to write her own romances for the enjoyment of herself and others. She's very excited about seeing her work in print and is thrilled to be the second Australian to write for the Silhouette Desire line.

Maxine lives in Melbourne, Australia, but over the years has traveled to New Zealand, the UK and the USA. In her own backyard, her husband's job ensured they saw the diversity of the countryside, including spending many years in Darwin in the tropical north where some of her books are set. She is married to Geoff, who has proven his hero-status many times over the years. They have two handsome sons and an assortment of much-loved, previously abandoned animals.

Maxine would love to hear from you and can be contacted through her Web site at www.maxinesullivan.com.

For Serena Tatti
Terrific Writer and Caring Friend
"One of the Best"

One

"We meet at last, Mrs. Ford," Flynn Donovan drawled, looking into a pair of heart-stopping, exquisitely arresting blue eyes. In that instant, *he wanted her*. With a passion as absurd as it was unexpected.

For a moment the woman appeared startled, then whatever she saw made her delicate chin rise and her delicious mouth tighten. "I'm sorry to disturb you…" she said coolly.

Disturb him? Hell, despite her poise, Danielle Ford radiated a sex appeal that reached out and grabbed him by the…throat.

"Mr. Donovan, you sent a letter demanding repayment of a loan my husband and I—"

Suddenly he was angry with her for being so damn gorgeous on the outside and so damn dishonest within.

He knew her type. Robert Ford had said his wife was superb at acting and that her "innocent" look could hook a man until she got all she could out of him. He wasn't fool enough to believe everything Robert Ford had said, but any woman married to that liar and cheat must be tarred with the same brush.

"Don't you mean your *late* husband?" he snapped, flicking his pen on the desk.

Her slim shoulders tensed, even as her eyes reflected surprise at his tone. "My *late* husband, then." She took a breath. "About the letter. It says I owe you two hundred thousand dollars but I have no idea what this is about."

"Come now, Mrs. Ford," he mocked. "What you actually thought was that you'd try and con your way out of repaying back the loan you took out from my company."

She gasped, her thick lashes blinking in confusion. "But I don't know anything about a loan. And certainly not for such an amount. There must be some mistake."

And he was supposed to believe that?

"Don't play dumb."

A blush stained her cheeks, making her appear oddly vulnerable.

Or guilty, but then, a person could only feel guilty if they had a conscience. He doubted this woman had one.

"I assure you I'm not playing dumb, Mr. Donovan."

His jaw clenched. "Is this the same assurance your husband gave us when he borrowed the money from one of my loan officers?" He pushed some papers across his desk toward her. "Isn't that your signature alongside your husband's?"

Her eyes clouded with apprehension as she took a few steps closer, before looking down at the paperwork.

Then she paled and sank onto a chair. "It *looks* like my signature but…" Her voice trailed away to nothing.

Oh, so that's how she was going to play it. Robert had been right about her. She wasn't about to admit to anything, not even when the evidence of her guilt was right in front of her.

"It *is* your signature, Mrs. Ford," he said, ignoring her "helpless female" act. "And now you owe me two hundred thousand dollars."

Her head snapped up, her eyes wide and panicked. "But I don't have that kind of money."

He knew that already. After some investigating he'd learned she had exactly five thousand dollars in the bank here in Darwin. The rest she'd flittered all away, as evidenced by a variety of empty accounts around the rest of Australia. He was beginning to feel sorry for that poor guy who'd married her. She'd turn any man's head.

God, she was beautiful.

And that body…

His gaze slid down her simple pink dress and matching jacket that made a soft statement of style, to the slender legs revealed by the hem of her dress.

Nice.

Very nice.

They'd look really sexy in a tub full of fluffy white bubbles, one shapely calf raised as she smoothed soap over its silky length, the water's edge just stopping short of covering her breasts. The image aroused him without any effort at all, sending the blood pounding through his veins, telling him he needed a woman.

This woman.

"Then perhaps we can come to a compromise?" he said, leaning back in his leather executive chair to watch her more closely.

Her eyelids gave the slightest flutter, before she angled her chin, as if daring him to take another look. For a moment he was tempted.

She pulled herself up straighter. "Maybe I can pay you back a little each week. It'll take a long time but—"

"Not good enough." There was only one payment he wanted now.

Her lips parted in surprise, their perfect bow shape too damn appealing. "Wh-what?"

"You'll have to do better than that, I'm afraid."

She hesitated, as if trying to understand. "I'm not sure—"

"You're a very beautiful woman, Mrs. Ford."

Her eyes held his for a heartbeat, then a pulse began to leap crazily in a tiny vein in her neck. "I've been widowed for two months, Mr. Donovan. Have you no sensibility?"

"Apparently not." He wanted to place his lips on that neck and feel her heart beating against him.

She let out a sigh. "Then you must tell me how I can repay you. I can certainly do with some money at the moment."

Ah, yes. Money is what it came down to with this woman. His gut knotted at the reminder of how mercenary she was.

"Sorry, sweetheart. You don't get another cent from me until you pay back the loan. In full."

Her cheekbones instantly reddened. "Oh, but I didn't mean—"

"Yes, you did."

She looked taken aback for just a moment, then quickly recovered. "Oh, yes, of course I did," she said with sarcasm. "I'll take as much money as I can get out of you. I'm good at that, you know."

As a bluff, it didn't work. He knew what she was trying to do. "Yes, you're very good at that."

She threw him a glare. "I'm glad you can read my mind. I hope you can read what I'm thinking right now?"

He felt a ripple of amusement. "A lady shouldn't know such words."

"A lady shouldn't have to sit here and listen to you blackmail her, either."

"*Blackmail* is an ugly word, Danielle." He rolled the name over in his mind the way he wanted to roll her over in bed. "I merely want what is mine."

And she was one of them.

Her lips pressed together briefly before she answered, "No, you want revenge. I'm sorry, but I can't be blamed for my husband's mistakes."

Flynn stared hard. "What about *your* mistakes, Danielle? You signed for the loan, didn't you? Therefore you are just as liable to pay me back."

"With my money or with my body?" she scoffed.

He arched a brow. "I wonder how many hot tropical nights two hundred thousand dollars is worth?" He thought for a moment, then answered his own question. "Hmm. About three months, I'd say." Expensive, yes, but he knew he'd pay that for just *one* night with this woman.

Her blue eyes turned disbelieving, as if only now realizing he was serious. "Three months! You expect me to *sleep* with you for *three* months?"

His gaze lingered on her mouth. So perfect. "I didn't say anything about sleeping with me, though I guarantee it wouldn't be a hardship," he said, as her surprisingly sensual fragrance wafted across the desk and slid into him, stirring his blood. "No, I have a lot of engagements coming up and I could do with a…mistress to accompany me."

Awareness flickered in the back of her eyes, then was quickly blanked out.

She got to her feet. "Mr. Donovan, you're dreaming if you think I'll give my time…or my body…to a man like you. Let me suggest you wake yourself up and find a woman who would actually welcome your company." With those words, she spun on her heels and left the office.

In cynical amusement, Flynn watched her go, then got to his feet and stood looking out the huge window of Donovan Towers to the sparkling expanse of harbor spread before him. He rather liked her response. It was a far cry from some of the females he'd been out with lately, who'd left him cold with their easy acquiescence to anything remotely connected to bedroom games.

And then he remembered.

Danielle Ford was more sinner than saint. Her token resistance was only a game, one she'd already played with her late husband. From what Robert Ford had said, she'd taken him on a wild ride during their marriage, though he doubted Robert had needed any encouragement. They had obviously deserved each other. No, he wouldn't forget she had belonged to Robert Ford and that the two of them had reneged on a loan. A pair well-matched.

He muttered a swearword and turned back to his desk, knowing he had a morning of video conferences with personnel in Sydney and Tokyo ahead of him, yet for once the thought of work didn't appeal. Not even the promise of a particularly satisfying takeover tomorrow.

He preferred instead another sort of takeover, with a woman who had gorgeous blue eyes and golden-blond hair and a willowy body.

Despite her protestations, he would make her his mistress. No doubt she would sell her soul for a chance to rub shoulders with him and his billions.

After catching a taxi home, Danielle still trembled from her encounter as she let herself into her air-conditioned apartment. She'd come to love living in this tropical paradise…this vibrant capital city at the top of Australia's Northern Territory…but now there was a serpent in paradise by the name of Flynn Donovan. God, he had to be deranged if he thought she would pay off her debts with her body.

Her debts.

She swallowed hard and sank down on the gray leather sofa, her knees suddenly weak. What had Robert been thinking when he'd forged her signature on that document? Because it *was* a forgery, that was certain. She even remembered when he'd tried to get her to sign some paperwork. He'd said it was a business deal and he needed her signature as a witness. Only she'd felt uncomfortable and *accidentally* misplaced it. She heard nothing more about it from Robert. Pity she hadn't read it before she'd thrown it away.

Two hundred thousand dollars! For what? It made her wonder what else he had done. Had she known her husband at all?

Not that Flynn Donovan would have believed her if she'd told him the truth. He clearly thought she was as guilty as her husband and any further attempt to refute that would have been met with suspicion.

She blinked back tears. This was supposed to be a new beginning for her. After three years of being smothered by Robert and his mother, she'd finally broken free after his death and moved into this luxury apartment. Living with her mother-in-law had been hard enough during her unhappy marriage, but since Robert's death, Monica had been trying to manipulate her, just as she had her "Robbie." And feeling sorry for the other woman's loss, she had given in too many times to count.

But eventually she'd had enough. A Realtor who'd been an acquaintance of Robert's had offered Danielle this penthouse at minimal rent. Signing the lease had lifted a lead weight from her shoulders. The place was beautiful and made her happy. She loved the spacious living room and open-plan kitchen, and the glass doors leading to the balcony looked over a wide expanse of ocean. Being surrounded by such beauty made her feel as if she could breathe again. It had been exactly what she'd needed, and better yet, it was all *hers*. For a year, anyway.

And now *this*.

Now she owed Donovan Enterprises a large sum of money and had no idea how she was going to pay it back. And pay it back she would. She just wouldn't feel right about it if she didn't. Robert had taken the money and she was Robert's wife and, as much as she wanted to walk away from it all and say it wasn't her problem, she couldn't. It *was* her problem.

But the five thousand dollars she'd managed to save from her part-time job was woefully inadequate. Besides, she wouldn't give that up. *Couldn't* give it up. It was her security blanket, held in an account Robert had known nothing about. Thank God. He hadn't wanted her to be independent, and she'd fought hard to hold on to her job during her marriage—against both Robert's and Monica's wishes. If she'd given it up to become a lady of leisure the way they'd wanted, then somehow she may as well have given up on herself.

No, she'd just have to find another way to pay the money back. And not through sleeping with Flynn, either, even though she couldn't deny her heart had skipped a beat over him.

The tycoon had definitely been at the front of the line when they were handing out good looks, with the sort of handsome features that stole a woman's breath and curled her toes.

Strong, silent and sexy. With broad shoulders more than enough for one woman to caress, not to mention the kind of thick dark hair that invited a woman's hands.

She could imagine feeling its shining silkiness beneath her fingertips.

Perhaps some would call her crazy for refusing to go to bed with a man with such remarkable dark eyes and a sensually molded mouth. She called it survival.

He was one of those men who expected everyone to do his bidding. She'd spent three years being smothered by a man who'd fought to control her and she wasn't about to step back into another relationship like that—no matter how much money Flynn Donovan said she owed.

Two

The next day Danielle had just bent to pick up some broken glass when the doorbell rang, making her cut herself on one of the pieces. Sucking in a sharp breath, she quickly drew back her hand, relieved to see the cut was only small. She already had a lump on her head where the heavy gold picture frame had toppled onto her as she'd been adjusting it.

But all that was forgotten when she opened the door and found the stunningly virile Flynn Donovan standing there, dressed in a dark business suit that fit his body as if it were a labor of love.

"I heard breaking glass," he said without preamble, his gaze taking in her orange-burst silk tunic over white pants, down to her white sandals, as if looking for injury. There was more in that look than necessary and she fought not to react. But her skin quivered anyway. That look was too seductive…too physical….

And then she remembered who this man was and what he wanted from her. At the very least he wanted money.

At the worst…

She forced aside her apprehension and shot him a cold look. "How did you get in the building? We have a security code, you know. It's supposed to keep out unwanted guests."

"I have my ways," he said, dismissively, with all the arrogance of someone rich enough to get anything he wanted. "The broken glass?" he reminded her.

She raised one slim shoulder. "A picture frame fell off the wall."

His eyes sharpened with a concern that was at odds with the forbidding set of his jaw. "Are you hurt?"

For a moment she was tempted to lie. "A small cut, that's all." Nonchalantly she lifted her finger to show him, but when she saw how much blood covered the tissue, she gasped.

He swore. "Danielle, that is no small cut," he muttered, reaching for her hand, his touch scorching her. She tried to pull back…tried not to welcome the feel of his skin against hers…but he held firm.

To counteract the effect, she glared at him. "I wouldn't have cut it at all if you hadn't rang the doorbell just as I was picking up the glass."

"Next time I'll leave you to bleed to death," he said brusquely, undoing the tissue to reveal the injured finger. He scowled as he examined it. "There's a lot of blood, but I think you'll get away without stitches." He raised his head, his dark eyes stabbing her. "Any other injuries I should know about?"

Tell him no.

But the truth slipped out. "Only a bump on the head."

"Show me."

She winced where she felt the lump. "It's nothing, really. It's—"

"Bleeding," he growled, moving in closer, touching her head.

She swallowed convulsively. "I'll be fine."

"Where's your first-aid kit?"

"In the kitchen, but—"

"Right." He cupped her elbow and started her forward with him. "Let's take a proper look at it."

Her skin continued to scorch where he touched. "Mr. Donovan, I'm sure you've got better things to do than play doctor with me," she said as they sidestepped the broken glass.

He shot her a masculine look that coiled tension inside her. His thoughts didn't need to be said out loud to fill the silence between them.

As soon as she reached the kitchen, she quickly moved away from him and took the small box out of a cupboard to place on the bench. He followed her, then began searching through the contents. Taking advantage of the moment, she stepped back, grateful the kitchen was large and airy and far less intimate than two people standing in a doorway.

"Move that stool over there and sit under the light," he ordered. "I'll be able to see better."

That was what she was afraid of. But, her heart thudding against her ribs, she did what he said anyway. Better to get it over and done with so he'd leave sooner rather than later.

He came toward her, the ball of cotton in his hand contrasting with the tan of his skin. And then he stood behind her, bringing a very male scent with him. She'd noticed it when he'd walked in but now the scent intensified like a potent wine, ready to lull her into blissful surrender.

She jumped when he brushed a lock of her blond hair aside and began dabbing at the cut. His touch was gentle yet probing, the way a man's touch should be. Would he be the same in bed? Oh, yes, he'd know how to turn a woman on.

"Mr. Donovan—"

"Flynn," he suddenly said in a rough voice.

She ignored that. "Mr. Donovan, I think—"

"How long will it take you to pack?"

That pulled her thoughts up short. "Pack?"

"For Tahiti. I have to go there for business. My jet's on standby. We can leave within the hour."

"Tahiti?" She spun to face him, barely wincing as his fingers brushed her scalp. Dear God, what was he saying?

His dark eyes watched her with a knowing look in them. "I have a house there. Our privacy will be assured."

It fell into place then. He expected her to go away with him as payment for the loan. God, did he really think she would do such a thing?

"I don't need any privacy," she choked, strangely hurt. "I don't intend to go away with you." A burst of anger hit her. "Anyway, just who do you think you are? You snap your fingers and I'm to drop everything?

Sorry. Your women friends may do that but I have a mind of my own."

His eyes hardened. "Oh, come now, Danielle. Who are you trying to fool?"

She straightened her shoulders. "The only fool around here is *you.*"

His face tightened, making her aware of the firm thrust of his jaw and the broad plane of his forehead. "Don't underestimate me."

A frisson of fear slipped down her spine. This man had wealth, power and the right connections and he believed she'd done him an injustice. As much as she wanted to deny he could make life uncomfortable for her, she knew he would do it if pushed. She couldn't afford that. There wasn't only herself to think about now.

She moistened her mouth and tried to be conciliatory. "Mr. Donovan, please... I don't sleep with men I barely know."

"That isn't what your late husband told me."

She felt the blood drain from her face.

"I see you don't like being caught out," he mocked, seeming to watch her more closely.

Pain squeezed her heart. Robert...her husband...the man she'd been married to for three years...had told Flynn Donovan such lies about her? Why?

"Um..." She cleared her throat. "What exactly did Robert say?"

"That you married him for his money. And that you slept around and spent it all," he said bluntly.

It was just as well she was sitting on the stool or she may well have fallen. How *could* Robert have said those things about her? She'd thought she'd loved Robert when she married him. And she never, ever slept around and she'd never wasted his money. *Never.*

Then she looked at Flynn Donovan. At that moment she hated Robert for his lies, but she hated Flynn more for his lack of compunction over her feelings. "I see. You obviously believed him."

His lips twisted. "When he explained the reason for defaulting on the loan, I wasn't actually concerned with character references."

"Yet you lent the money to us based on character," she said, her voice remarkably calm considering the turmoil inside her.

His eyes narrowed. "No, we based it on the fact that he was coming into money and would pay us back as soon as he received it. He seemed a good risk at the time. We didn't take into account that you had the money spent before he could even get to it."

Danielle remembered Robert mentioning something about coming into an inheritance from one of his aunts, but she hadn't realized it was a large enough amount to serve as collateral for a loan. For him to have then spent that amount plus the two hundred thousand he'd borrowed from Flynn Donovan spoke of sheer irresponsibility.

And Monica? Had she known? Danielle didn't think so. Her mother-in-law was well-off in her own right but had never discussed money and, in any case, she knew Monica had never suspected her son had a problem with money.

She certainly hadn't suspected any problems, Danielle mused as she realized Flynn had walked over to the first-aid kit and was rummaging around in it. One thing was clear. No one would believe her if she chose to refute Robert's claims.

"Why deny it?" Flynn said coldly over his shoulder, confirming her fears. "Your car alone cost fifty thousand dollars, not to mention your frequent European holidays and shopping sprees. Your credit cards were maxed to the limit, too."

Credit cards? European holidays? Shopping sprees? She fought to take it all in. Had someone stolen her identity? It certainly hadn't been *her* doing all those things. Robert had been the one to…

Oh, God. Is that what Robert had been doing on his frequent business trips? The ones where he'd wanted her to stay home as company for his mother?

As for the car, she'd had no idea of its cost. Robert had always seemed to have plenty of money and as far as she'd known, the car had been in his name only. He definitely hadn't insured it. Or himself. If only he had, she could at least have paid back some of the money now.

And then something occurred to her. The holidays, the shopping, didn't sound like something one did alone. Had Robert been unfaithful to her? Looking back, she knew he was selfish enough to want his cake and eat it, too. What sort of double life had he been living? And why didn't that thought hurt as much as it should?

Suddenly she realized Flynn was in front of her, bringing her into the present with a rush. In that moment they were right back to one man, one woman.

Her heart gave a sudden lurch when he picked up her

finger and covered it with the antiseptic cream before placing a plaster around it. The gentleness of his touch confused her. How could he be tender in one aspect and so hardhearted in another?

But she wasn't about to show him her uncertainty. He would take advantage of it. "Mr. Donovan, you think I want you for your money, yet you're willing to take me away with you? That doesn't make sense."

"It makes perfect sense," he murmured, his throaty tone faint but potent. "We were meant to spend time together."

"Of all the..." She almost jumped to her feet but that would have brought her closer to him and at the last millisecond she stopped herself. His eyes darkened at how close she'd come to being in his arms.

She leveled him a look. "Don't let me keep you," she said, but cursed her husky voice and refused to allow the tip of her tongue to moisten her suddenly dry lips.

He cupped her chin with his warm fingers, holding her head still, as if he wanted to wet her lips for her. "You won't," he said huskily, his eyes intent on her mouth.

His head began to lower. She lifted her face up to him...ready...ready to become *his*.

And then he moved imperceptibly closer, and the movement broke through the fog of desire that seemed to swirl around them.

His? Dear God, what was she thinking? She never wanted to belong to another man again.

And definitely not Flynn Donovan.

She pulled her head back. "There is no way I'm going away with you," she murmured, shaken at how close she'd come to kissing him.

Something flickered far back in those dark eyes before they flashed a now-familiar display of arrogance. "Is that so?" To prove his point, he lifted some strands of her hair from her cheek and tugged her toward him.

She held her head still, refusing to wince at the slight pain, unwilling to let him force her into submission. She wasn't going to become his plaything. She couldn't, despite the desire coursing through her.

"Do you think you could leave now?" she said coolly, determined not to let him see his effect on her. "I'm expecting a…" She paused deliberately. "Friend."

He let her strands of hair drop back into place and drawled mockingly, "You have no…friend."

"You don't know that."

"Perhaps I've been checking up on you?" He smiled in satisfaction when she jumped. "But that's not how I know. A man just knows these things. You tremble when I touch you…." He touched her cheek. "See."

She jerked her head away. "With revulsion."

He gave a hard laugh. "That's a new one. No woman has ever told me that before."

"Then you'd better get used to it."

"Why? Do you expect I'll touch you a lot?" he mocked but his voice had a raw edge. His eyes raked over her. "No, *you* had better get used to the trembling. I intend to make you…tremble…often."

She inwardly trembled now. "Stop playing games."

"Oh, but the games have only just begun," he said silkily. "You owe me money and I *will* collect."

"Wh-what? *Now?*"

He seemed to take inventory of each feature on her face. "No. I'd rather wait and savor you in my own time, at my own pace."

She felt as if her breath was cut off. "I'm not a delicacy to be enjoyed."

"Really? I think you'd be very good in small bites."

She snorted. "I would give you food poisoning."

"Aah, but I'd enjoy myself first." A sardonic gleam of amusement entered his eyes. "Just like you. Spend now, pay later. That's your motto, isn't it?" Without warning, one brow lifted with cynicism. "I wonder how many other people you've tried to cheat?"

She went rigid. She'd never tried to cheat anyone in her life. She'd always considered herself dependable and loyal. Even with Robert, she'd stayed with him because she'd believed in her marriage vows.

Of course, she hadn't known Robert had taken his vows less than seriously in return.

"Nothing to say?"

These allegations had gone on long enough. She had to make him see sense. Yesterday she'd been shocked by his accusations and hadn't really believed he intended to make her his lover.

But now…today…with him coming here…with his jet ready for Tahiti…she couldn't let this sham go on.

Yet, dare she tell him? Would it make him even angrier with her when he knew he couldn't have her? *Why* he couldn't have her? Would he get spiteful, the way Robert used to when he didn't get his own way?

She drew herself up without actually getting off the stool. "Mr. Donovan—"

"Flynn."

"Flynn," she said, conceding just this once. "I'm sorry, but there is no way I can share your bed."

"You can't, eh? And why would that be?" Thankfully he moved back to lean against the sink, but the sheer insolence in his stance made her heart dip. It was obvious he thought she was just being difficult for the sake of it.

Still, she had to try. She slipped off the stool, automatically arching her spine, her silky top a river of orange as it flowed into place over her white slacks. Her back was aching a little lower down but she hoped that was to be expected.

Then she heard him suck in a breath. "My God! Are you pregnant?"

Danielle straightened, shocked that he'd guessed the truth even though she wasn't showing. And suddenly she was aware that her actions had spoken louder than words. Perhaps that wasn't a bad thing. Hopefully for him to see that she was going to be a mother would be more effective than all the words in the world.

He raised his eyes to her face and there was a terrible pain in them that tugged at her heartstrings. She wasn't sure why, but her hands went to her stomach, protectively. "Um…that's what I wanted to tell you."

He stood there for a long moment. Staring… And then he pushed himself upright and away from the sink, his body rigid, his mouth curling with contempt. "*Now* I see what this is all about," he rasped. "No wonder you wouldn't fall into bed with me. You wanted more, just like your husband said you did with him."

She blinked. "More?"

"A marriage license to be exact."

Shock ran through her. "You're crazy," she managed to say, if a little unsteadily. She wouldn't be thinking about marriage again. Not for a long time.

"You've gone through one husband's money—" the words hit her like bullets "—and now you're trying to tie yourself to another. What better way to get sympathy than to play the grieving but pregnant widow without a penny to her name? Poor, beautiful Danielle," he sniped at her in a harsh voice. "Most men would give up their freedom to possess you, and being pregnant makes you even more attractive to some. There's something dignified about having a wife with child." His angry gaze swept over her. "Is it even your husband's baby?"

She felt sick with the horror of it all. "I resent you asking, but, yes, it's my husband's baby." His mocking words echoed in her mind. "Or should I say my *late* husband's baby."

"Did he know?"

It wasn't any of Flynn's business but she inclined her head anyway. Robert had been ecstatic, for which she was grateful, no matter what she was finding out about him now. She hadn't wanted a child until things had improved between them, but somehow she must have missed taking her contraceptive pill one time and she'd fallen pregnant.

Naturally she'd been fearful at first, not because the child would go unloved, but because Monica and Robert loved in a smothering way. But she knew she was strong enough to keep that in check and she had even begun to welcome her pregnancy. Her baby would bring some happiness back into their lives.

And it still would, she told herself, feeling Flynn's eyes burning into her.

Ignoring the pain of insult, she raised her chin. "Mr. Donovan, let me make one thing clear to you. I have no intention of looking for a surrogate father for my baby." She paused for effect. "And even if I was, I'd never pick someone like you. My baby deserves more than someone with a checkbook for a heart."

He walked toward her, his dark eyes without a glimmer of kindness. "Don't presume to know me, lady. If that was my child growing in your belly you wouldn't have a choice." With those words, he stormed past her and out of the apartment.

Eyes misting over, Danielle just stood there as the door slammed behind him, a terrible ache in her breast, her thoughts in turmoil. Never in a million years would she have believed all this could be happening to her.

Yesterday morning she hadn't even met Flynn Donovan. She'd assumed his letter about the money was a mistake. Now she'd been accused not only of cheating on her husband and abusing his money, but of being a calculating schemer who wanted nothing but a rich man to play father to her child. It was clear he had far from a high opinion of her.

Well, she didn't have one of him, either. He may

be one of the richest men in Australia but as far as she was concerned he could keep his money and his private jet and…and…

She swiped at her tears. What did it matter now, anyway? The way Flynn had stormed out of here left her in no doubt he wouldn't be back. No, he'd be putting the debt collectors onto her now. They'd be hounding her like a pack of dogs after a bone.

She took a shaky breath. He needn't bother. She'd find a way to pay the money back. How could she enjoy her independence knowing that her late husband had "stolen" the money, not just from Flynn but from Donovan Enterprises, as well?

And she had too much to lose if she didn't.

Oh, God. Suddenly it hit her that the debt collectors would go talk to Monica. And if the older woman became aware of the loan, she would use it to get custody of the baby. Oh, dear God, she would. Danielle was never more certain of anything in her life. Her mother-in-law wanted…no, *needed* someone to replace her son…and who better than Robert's unborn child?

And if Flynn Donovan believed she'd defaulted on the money, then Monica would, too, and could make a case for Danielle being an unfit mother, and probably with Flynn's help. After all, how did she prove that it *hadn't* been her signature? Her mother-in-law only needed a sympathetic judge…or a corrupt one.

Danielle's heart squeezed so tightly with pain it felt as if it had wedged under her rib cage. She couldn't take the risk of losing her child, no matter how slender.

Three

Life rarely took Flynn by surprise anymore, but when it did, he didn't like it one bit. Danielle Ford was pregnant. Hell! He didn't want to get involved with a pregnant woman. Anything could happen to a woman when she was pregnant.

It had happened to his mother.

He could still remember his mother's voice calling to him where he'd been playing in the backyard under the mango tree with his friends Brant and Damien.... The same mango tree that still stood a few suburbs away from here. He'd come inside the house and found her on the floor, covered in blood.

"The baby's coming," she'd said, her face screwed up in pain. "Go get Auntie Rose."

More terrified than he'd ever been in his five-year-old life, he'd run next door with his friends as fast as his little legs had allowed. After that it had been a whirl of people running and sirens screaming. And all the while, he'd stood in the background, watching his mother's life slipping away…away from him.

He hated thinking about it, and as always he shut his mind off and pushed aside the past. He had to concentrate on the here and now, and that no longer included Danielle Ford. She could forget about the money she owed him. Forget about it and go find some other poor sucker to con with those "come-to-bed" eyes and that "give-me-your-money" mouth. As far as he was concerned, Danielle Ford no longer existed.

It was just a pity that spending the following weekend in Sydney at his apartment overlooking the million-dollar view of the Harbor Bridge and Opera House wouldn't be enjoyable. Something was missing.

Or someone.

Dammit, he'd never let a woman get under his skin before. Not like this. He'd had women friends who'd tried every trick in the book to get him to marry them, but Danielle Ford had chosen a different way of getting his attention. Unfortunately for her it had the opposite effect to what she'd wanted. The one thing he wouldn't let himself do was get involved with a pregnant woman.

Not that pregnant women weren't beautiful. He'd seen some stunners in his time and thankfully none had been his responsibility, but he'd decided years ago he'd never put any woman's life at risk with a pregnancy.

So why couldn't he get this one woman out of his mind, especially since he *hadn't* taken her to his bed?

Or perhaps it was because of that?

Yet she was only one woman. There were plenty of others to choose from. But those women would only have been a poor substitute for a sexy sorceress…a witch…but a cheat, he reminded himself.

He had to stop thinking about a certain long-legged, blue-eyed blonde stripped naked and in bed….

His bed…

He wasn't surprised the following week after returning from a business lunch with the Lord Mayor when his personal assistant followed him into his office, an angry look on her middle-aged face. Connie rarely lost her cool. It was one of the things he appreciated about her. She kept calm under the most trying of circumstances.

Usually.

"This was delivered downstairs at reception," she said tightly, slapping an envelope down on the desk in front of him. "It's for *you*."

He leaned back in his chair, his eyes narrowing, not sure what it was about. "And?"

A disapproving motherly look puckered her lips. "It's from Mrs. Ford."

"Danielle?" he said, tensing, and caught the suddenly watchful look in his assistant's eyes at his slip of the tongue.

"Yes."

He wondered what Danielle was up to now, even as mild surprise at Connie's reaction filled him. "You didn't like her?"

A soft look filled her eyes. "Of course I liked her, Flynn. She's lovely. So well-mannered." Then her expression tightened again as she shot him daggers. "You had better read the letter, that's all I'm saying."

Hiding his wariness, he merely inclined his head. "Thank you, Connie. Just leave it there."

She looked as if she was going to say more, but then obviously knowing how far *not* to push him, she left the room, closing the door behind her.

For a moment Flynn just sat there, marshaling his thoughts. He stared at the open white envelope. His name had been written on it in a soft style that bespoke of femininity and charm. The uppercase initials of *F* and *D* fashioned with little curls tugged on something inside him, as if it were an echo of her voice wanting him.

God, he could still hear the throaty sound of her voice back in her kitchen when he'd been administering to her injuries.

Didn't this woman know when to give up?

Never one to shirk anything unpleasant, he seized the envelope and pulled out the folded piece of paper inside. He began to read.

Dear Mr. Donovan,
Please find enclosed a check for one hundred dollars as first payment on the outstanding loan of two hundred thousand dollars that my late husband and I owe your company. I apologize if this is unacceptable, however due to my pregnancy I am unable to take a second job at this stage. Please

take this as official notice that I will repay the loan
as soon as I can.
Yours sincerely,
Danielle Ford.

Flynn threw the letter on his desk, his lips twisting
at the word *sincerely*. No wonder Connie had been upset
with him. Danielle's words might have been business-
like in tone but it made him sound like an ogre who was
insisting on his money, come hell or high water.

Obviously this was the way she worked. And now
the pregnancy angle had added a whole new avenue to
her manipulation skills. She'd certainly hit the jackpot
with that one.

As for her "supposed" job, it was probably some
sort of volunteer work she did once a month at the hospital. Something that made her look respectable without
getting her pretty little hands dirty, he decided, tearing
up the check and dropping the pieces in the wastepaper
basket.

No doubt once he ignored this, they wouldn't be
hearing from her again. Her little ploy for sympathy
would soon die a natural death once she realized he
wasn't about to come running with a magic wand in one
hand and an unlimited checkbook in the other.

Then the same thing happened the following week.
A check arrived, but without a letter this time.

"Another check," Connie said tightly, slapping the
envelope down in front of him, as if everything were *his*
fault. She smacked another piece of paper on top of it
and blurted, "And here's my resignation."

His head snapped up. "Your *what?*" He didn't wait for her to answer. "What the— Why?"

She straightened her slim shoulders, color coming into her cheeks. "I'm afraid I can't work for you anymore, Flynn. Not like this."

He exhaled an impatient sigh and leaned back in his chair. *This* was Danielle Ford's fault. Damn her. And damn Danielle's flashing blue eyes, those enticing lips above the intimate underside of a chin that more often than not was raised in the air at him.

"So you're going to throw away five years of working for me because some…" he hesitated to say *lady* "…woman owes me money?"

"Yes."

From his experience he knew females were often unpredictable, but he'd never actually thought of Connie that way. She'd been his right-hand man, always on top of things, never one to pull these kinds of tricks.

"She's not worth it, you know."

Connie met his gaze levelly. "I think she is. She's a real lady, Flynn. Classy. She deserves better than this."

No, Danielle was just good at fooling people, though he had to admit that not many people fooled Connie. And that just went to prove that his assistant wasn't infallible.

"She owes me a great deal of money," he pointed out.

Connie continued to stand her ground. "I'm sure she had her reasons."

His mouth thinned with derision. "That means she *spent* a great deal of money, or hadn't you thought of that?"

"I don't care. A pregnant woman shouldn't have to worry about getting a second job to pay the bills."

"Then maybe she shouldn't have borrowed the money in the first place."

Her expression was resolute. "That may be so, but she's genuinely trying to pay the money back now." A wave of concern crossed her face. "Look, her husband is dead, she's pregnant and she has a debt that is obviously weighing heavily on her. It could affect her health."

"No," he growled. He wasn't going to have *that* on his shoulders.

Connie hesitated for a second, then a determined look filled her eyes. "Flynn, I never told you this before but I was pregnant once."

His brows met in a frown. They'd never discussed her private life. She worked long hours at times and had never complained, so he assumed she lived alone.

"You never mentioned being married."

"I wasn't." Her eyes didn't waver from his. "I hope that doesn't change how you think of me."

"That's a fool thing to say," he said brusquely. "Of course it doesn't make a bloody difference."

Her features relaxed with slight relief. "Thank you," she murmured, but there was inner pain flickering at the back of her eyes. "Let me tell you a little about my baby. I lost him before he was born. You see, I'd been in poor health for some years, I had no family and the man I loved had left town before he even knew I was pregnant. I thought I was too proud to accept charity, but when you lose your baby…" her voice grew slightly shaky "…when that baby no longer warms your womb and you have nothing in your arms to hold…" She took another breath. "Accepting charity suddenly looks the better option."

The world briefly shifted out of focus as memories of his mother rose to the surface again.

Then he looked at his PA. To think Connie had gone through a similar thing…

His mouth firmed with purpose. "Put your resignation away, Connie. I'll go see her."

Of course, he couldn't just drop everything right there and then, but a few hours later after moving a mountain of paperwork, he eventually left to go see Danielle, the loan contract tucked inside his jacket. He knew he was playing right into her hands by coming to see her, but how to tell his PA that? The first check and accompanying letter had been a brilliant idea, but the second check was sheer stubbornness. It was obvious Danielle was determined to get his attention.

And he was equally determined not to give it. Not in the way she wanted, anyway.

Still, she wouldn't be complaining too loudly once he'd finished talking. He was about to officially cancel the loan, thereby letting her walk away with two hundred thousand of his dollars. Not a bad day's work for some.

However the first thing he saw when he turned his sports Mercedes into her street was the reckless idiot in a red sedan who cut across the road and slammed on his brakes in front of her building.

Flynn swore as he pulled up behind the car and turned off the engine.

Bloody hell! Danielle was in that car. In the passenger seat. He'd recognize her profile anywhere.

And then he saw the young thug in the driver's seat next to her, his tattooed arm leaning out the window. Fear for her safety chilled his blood. The young man looked as if he'd just got out of prison, and the vehicle as if it had been driven by one too many drunks. The trunk of the car had a huge scratch down the middle and the back left-hand side had a dent in it the size of Kakadu National Park. There was a For Sale sign on its back window.

He swore again. Why on earth would she get into a car with such a man? She didn't belong there. It made his skin crawl just to see her sitting inside it.

And why buy that piece of garbage? She lived in a lavish penthouse apartment for God's sake, with a mesmerizing view of the marina and the vast Timor Sea beyond that. A view that even the most jaded would appreciate.

And then he figured out what she was *really* up to. She'd known he'd come here this afternoon and had somehow planned this, waiting in the afternoon heat and humidity, wanting him to feel sorry for her over the car and her condition. She'd probably counted on charming her way into his life. His nostrils flared with fury. She had about as much chance of that as of it snowing here in Darwin.

He was about to start the engine and go back to the office when he remembered his promise to Connie. If he went back now without speaking to Danielle, the older woman would hand in her notice. And then it would take too much time and trouble to find anyone half as efficient, let alone that he'd darn well miss her around the office.

Just then Danielle opened the car door and started to get out of the vehicle. Against his will, his pulse shifted upward when he glimpsed a pair of slim ankles encased in pretty white sandals more suited to getting out of a Mercedes than a run-down wreck. But it was the other car door being flung open and the jerky way the driver got out of the car that suddenly drew his attention.

Something was going on here.

Something not right.

Instinct told him this wasn't part of Danielle's plan.

Danielle had just been for the ride of her life. Not only was her stomach still trying to catch up from where "Turbo" had left it back there on a lonely stretch of the Stuart Highway, but her heart was still in her mouth. Living up to his name, he'd scared her half to death by crossing the other side of the road then coming to a screaming stop in front of her building.

Holding on to her stomach, she took a breath and opened the car door. Nothing would make her buy this car now, no matter how cheap. Her dear mother had always said you got what you paid for, and Danielle wasn't about to use some of her precious savings just to drive her baby around in a bomb like this one. She'd rather catch the bus into the city center the way she did now, where she worked three days a week helping Angie in the boutique. Of course, once she had the baby she'd need to stop at the day-care center before and after work.

"I'm sorry, but this really isn't what I'm looking for." She pushed herself off the passenger seat, wanting to get out of the car and away from this man who was making her uneasy.

He hopped out of the driver's side and looked at her over the roof of the car as she got to her feet. "I could probably take a couple of hundred off the price," he said, desperation growing in his tone.

She didn't want to think what he needed the money for. There was something about him that didn't sit well now. Heavens, she'd been a fool to get in the car with him, no matter that Angie said he was a friend of a friend.

"It's really not what I'm after, Turbo," she said in a placating tone.

"But you said—"

"The lady said she's not interested." A hard male voice came out of nowhere, and Danielle's gaze flew to the man standing a few feet away on the footpath. She sucked in a sharp breath, her heart hammering foolishly for one brief second. Flynn Donovan stood there, looking as if he wanted to do someone harm.

And that someone was probably *her*.

Turbo spun around, his mouth closing when he saw Flynn. All at once the young man appeared even skinnier and shorter, especially up against Flynn's well-muscled body dressed in a gray business suit.

Funny, but she actually felt sorry for Turbo then. The tattoos, the pierced nose and the missing tooth were merely a front so that people wouldn't notice his acne and too-thin body.

Flynn took a step closer and any suspicions she had about Turbo being up to no good disappeared under Flynn's intimidating stance. She glowered at him. Couldn't he see the younger man was nothing more than skin and bones?

"Flynn, don't—"

"Forget it, lady," Turbo interjected, his eyes wide with fright as he jumped in his car, gunned the engine and sped off, leaving behind a trail of exhaust smoke that sickened her in the humid tropical air.

But Danielle ignored it and glared at Flynn. "There was no need for that."

Reciprocating anger flared in those dark eyes. "Of course there was."

She bristled, half-afraid he was right but not willing to admit she'd acted foolishly. Not when she'd been trying so hard to do this all by herself.

Her chin tilted. "I could have handled him."

He arched a brow. "Really? It may have escaped your notice but you're pregnant."

"I know a man's weak parts as well as the next woman."

"Obviously." His mocking gaze traveled down the length of her floral shirt and white capri pants to the white sandals on her feet. For all his anger, she felt as if he'd just whispered kisses all down her body, right down to the tips of her toes.

Her hands balled into fists. "Mr. Donovan, just because I'm pregnant doesn't mean I'm helpless."

"Glad to hear it," he taunted.

She squared her shoulders. "Oh, I get it. You're one of those men who can't help but interfere in a woman's business. Well, I'd appreciate it if you'd stay out of mine in the future."

"Oh, I intend to." He started walking toward her, a dark glitter in his eyes. "After this."

She watched him warily. "What are you doing?"

Another two strides and he had her by the arm. "Getting you off the road before you get run over," he muttered, then started leading her back toward the building. "Or is that considered interfering, too?"

She was about to reply with something equally sarcastic, but all at once a funny feeling washed over her. Her head began to swim and, just as she reached the footpath, she felt the blood drain from her face and her knees turn weak. She clutched at Flynn with her other hand. God, she felt strange. Very, very strange. It must be the heat.

Suddenly both fear and panic that she'd done something to hurt the baby came crushing down on top of her. She took deep, calming breaths. *No,* she and the baby would be all right. It'll pass in a moment or two. She only had to wait.

"Danielle?" he said sharply.

She moistened dry lips. "I'm okay. I feel a little faint, that's all."

He muffled something under his breath.

"I should be fine now," she said in a small voice, and pushed herself away from him, but was unsteady on her feet.

He swore again and slipped his arms around her waist. "Let's get you upstairs."

Swinging her up in his arms, he punched in the security code he'd memorized from his last visit to the luxurious penthouse and headed inside to the coolness of the building. The elevator was available and he strode over plush carpet and into it, the lump of fear in his throat almost strangling him.

It was *her* he should strangle, he decided, as she rested her cheek on his shoulder, the soft fragrance of her perfume surrounding his nostrils. She didn't make a murmur.

Once inside her air-conditioned apartment, he laid her down on the leather couch in the living room, noting the faint sheen of perspiration covering her soft, almost translucent skin.

"Stay there," he grated, and headed for the telephone.

She lifted her head off the cushion. "What are you doing?"

He began punching in the first digits of the phone number. "Calling my doctor."

"What? Don't you dare!" She started to sit up, and he slammed the phone down and strode back to her side.

"You need medical attention," he growled, helping her to sit up fully. She was so light, even with the baby growing inside her.

The baby! Alarm rocketed through him again until he saw some color had returned to her cheeks.

"It was the smell of the exhaust fumes, that's all," she said, brushing some blond strands out of her eyes.

Powerful relief filled him, followed by a burst of irritation. How could she take this so casually? He hated to think what may have happened if he hadn't decided to come here today. No one would have heard her screams if that thug had roughed her up a little.

Or a lot.

He straightened, then impaled her with a stare. "You were taking your life in your hands with that idiot back there."

The pink in her cheeks reddened defensively. "His name was given to me by a friend."

His lip curled. "Terrific. The police will know exactly where to go *after* they find your mutilated body in Darwin Harbor. That's if the crocodiles don't get you first."

"Ever thought about writing bedtime books for children?" she mocked, sounding almost back to normal, if there even *was* such a thing as normal for her. She was the most ambiguous woman he'd ever met.

And he was in no mood to appreciate a sense of humor right now. "People don't always go around with Murderer tattooed on their foreheads."

She stirred uneasily, her beautiful face clouding over. "I wouldn't have gone with him if I'd really felt threatened. I have my baby to protect."

Flynn's eyes were drawn to where her hand rested on her stomach. He swallowed tightly, his gaze moving up and resting back on her face as he squashed the urge to pull her into his arms.

"That guy wouldn't have taken no for an answer," he

reiterated, knowing that if he got her in his arms he would shake her first. Then kiss her.

Fear came and went in her eyes. "I know that now."

Some of the tension eased out of his shoulders but he still couldn't let go of the suspicion that she'd do something foolish.

"Why are you here, Flynn?"

Absorbed in his angry thoughts, it was the sound of his name on her lips that broke through to him.

But it was her words that reminded him of the paperwork inside his jacket... Reminded him that she'd do almost anything to get his attention. This was all about getting her own way. She was definitely high maintenance—in more ways than one.

He smiled unpleasantly. "I've come to give you something."

She blinked warily. "You have?"

He took the contract out of his jacket and tossed it onto the sofa next to her. "Consider the loan paid in full. You no longer owe me two hundred thousand dollars."

For one moment something flashed in her eyes, before she quickly looked confused. "I don't understand."

He watched her with cynicism. He'd seen her eyes lit up with what he suspected was satisfaction. "Of course you do. Your letter...the checks...the run-down car...were all a bid for sympathy to get my attention and win me over. Why not just admit it?"

Her eyes flared wide. "What?"

"I'm one step ahead of you." He glanced pointedly at the paperwork. "Go on, pick it up and take a look. It's the contract. You can rip it up or burn it. Do what you will for all I care, but let's just cut our losses and get on with our lives. Separately."

Her delicious mouth opened and closed. Then, as if pretending she couldn't believe it, she looked down at the paper next to her and slowly picked it up. Her hands shook slightly and Flynn pushed aside a stab of guilt. They shook because he knew what she was about. He was probably the first man to so quickly see through her beautiful exterior to the hard core of selfishness beneath. Pregnant or not, this beauty intended to have it all.

Suddenly her head lifted and a deep anger bounced around in her blue eyes, surprising him.

"My God! I'm doing everything in my power to pay back the loan, and not only do you throw my effort back in my face but you accuse me of *subterfuge*."

Oh, she was convincing, but her actions spoke louder than words. She was angry because he'd caught her out. Her wealthy appetite was never more apparent than now, here in her expensive apartment.

He gave her a sweeping glance. "I know women."

She made a choking sound. "What a colossal ego you have."

"Then tell me how wrong I am about you," he said bluntly. "Tell me how you can afford an apartment like this—" he jerked his head at their swish surroundings "—yet not a decent car?"

A look of discomfort crossed her beautiful face before she tossed him a look full of sarcasm. "What? You mean you don't already know everything about my finances?"

She was as guilty as hell and disgust flooded through

him. She cried poor yet could afford to move into this? Perhaps he needed to get a new report done on her, and not just her business affairs this time.

"No doubt you have a lover or ex-lover paying most of your bills. What's the matter? Did you overspend and now he won't buy you a new car? Too bad."

"Think what you like," she said coolly.

"Oh, I will."

She flung him a look of intense dislike. "By the way, you can take your offer and…" Without warning, her voice wobbled and she blinked rapidly.

"Yes?" he taunted.

She cleared her throat. "Mr. Donovan, no matter what you say, I intend to pay the loan back, even if it takes me a lifetime."

He felt a flash of admiration, until he remembered this was just another ploy to trick him into believing she had integrity. She'd fooled Robert Ford at first, too.

All at once he wondered how far she would go in her quest to live the good life. How mercenary could she be? Would she take a new car if he offered it? He rather liked the idea of proving himself right. And dammit, he wasn't a charity but he couldn't bear to think of her pregnant self in a vehicle like he'd just seen. There would be no smooth ride in that thing.

He smiled with derision. If there was one thing she was used to it was a smooth ride, he decided, watching her sit back on the sofa like the lady of leisure she was, the contract casually resting on her lap.

Pushing aside his fanciful thoughts, he briefly glanced at his watch, noting the time. He had a half hour to get back to his office to meet with a visiting dignitary from overseas. What he really felt like doing was getting on his yacht and going for a sail along the coastline, letting the majestic view and cool sea breeze ease the tension out of his body. A tension that one woman had put there.

And still did.

He strode toward the door, but as he reached for the handle he suddenly pictured Danielle fainting. And what if she couldn't get up? She'd have to crawl to the telephone. Perhaps she'd be unable to do even that.

He opened the door then turned to look at her over his shoulder. "Do yourself a favor and get a cell phone." His gaze slid down to her stomach then back up again. "You never know when you'll need it."

Apprehension wavered in her eyes, then one of her eyebrows rose mockingly. "Gee, I wonder what pregnant women did before cell phones."

The muscles at the back of his neck bunched together as he glared at her. "Good question," he rasped, and shut the door on the way out.

Four

Everything about Flynn Donovan was so intense that Danielle brushed off his comment about pregnant women and cell phones. She had no idea why he'd accused her of ripping him off for not paying back the money for the loan, then turned right around and canceled it. Not that she had any intention of accepting the offer, as much as she'd wanted to take him up on it for just a split second. Oh, no. There would be conditions attached no matter what he said. As it was, she'd rather eat dirt.

But when a new shiny green sedan arrived courtesy of Donovan Enterprises, she was both stunned and dismayed. Could he know it was her birthday? Even if he did, why on earth would he make such a gesture? He couldn't get her into bed now. He'd made it more than clear he didn't *want* to get her into bed now. Why spend even more money on her if he didn't want something in return? It just didn't make sense.

But during the drive to his office to give the car back, a horrible suspicion occurred to her. Was he like Robert and wanted to play nasty little games with her? Robert had been spiteful when he didn't get his own way and would have done something like this just to make her suffer.

Was this Flynn's way of being spiteful because he couldn't have her in his bed? Did it give him some sort of satisfaction pretending to terminate the loan, then committing her to a new car so that she was still tied to him?

It had to be. She could think of no other reason a man would throw away good money, especially when he'd already made it clear he didn't give a damn about her as a person.

Thankfully his assistant wasn't at her desk, giving Danielle the opportunity to walk into Flynn's office without knocking.

He looked up from some paperwork, his eyes showing mild surprise, but she didn't give him the chance to speak. "I don't understand you," she said, walking toward him. "You accuse me of taking your money yet you want to spend more on me?" She slapped the car keys down on some papers. "No thanks. You can keep your money and your car. I don't need your help. I can manage to buy a car all by myself."

"Really?" His lips twisted. "You're not doing a very good job of it from what I can see."

Her cheeks filled with angry warmth. "Thanks for the compliment."

"Oh, so it's compliments you want, not my concern over the safety of you and your child. Or do you really want to drive around in a death trap like the one you were in yesterday?"

A shudder went through her. "You really know how to play dirty, don't you?"

"It's come in handy over the years."

She just bet it had.

He leaned back in his leather chair. "Why are you being so difficult about this?"

She clenched her teeth. "Why not? Isn't that how I get your *attention?*" she said sarcastically.

He straightened, a sudden icy contempt flashing in his eyes. "Look, you wanted a car, you've got one."

She lifted her chin. "I didn't ask."

"I didn't say you did. But you'll accept it, anyway. Well?" he proceeded.

She'd like to throw it back in his face but couldn't afford to right now. Instead, trying to gather her thoughts, she put her purse down on the desk and took a few steps over to the tropical fish tank next to the wall. For a couple of moments she watched the colorful array of fish swimming around in the clear water and felt an affinity with them. No matter how you looked at it, they were trapped.

Like she was.

Dear God, could she swallow her pride and refuse the car? Worse, could she risk her baby's life by buying a cheaper one that was perhaps not as safe?

Suddenly she knew what she had to do and she gave an inner groan. It would be hard but somehow she'd manage.

She turned to look at him. "I'll accept it on one condition. I'll pay it off, along with the other loan."

"Of course you will," he mocked.

Her eyes widened. "You don't believe me?"

"What's to believe? I've already told you to forget the money."

"And I said I'll accept the car, but I *won't* agree to not paying back the loan," she pointed out.

"Don't make a song and dance about it," he said, but there was a tiny muscle jerking at the corner of his mouth. "You're not fooling anyone but yourself if you think I can't see what you're about."

She pushed aside a sense of hurt. Once again she was being accused of something unpleasant. He thought all this was just a pretense on her part…that her objection was just lip service and she was actually reveling in him giving her a valuable car. It was obvious he expected her to take what she could get out of him.

"You're a fine one to talk. You're obviously doing this for your own sick reasons that have nothing to do with *me* but everything to do with *you*."

"Is that right?" he drawled, but she saw an alert look in his eyes.

"You want to hold it over my head, don't you? It makes you feel important to know that it will take me a lifetime to pay the loan back."

"I don't need you to make me feel important."

"Not from where I'm standing."

His mouth tightened. "I don't play games."

"Unlike me, you mean?"

"You said it."

That did it. She'd had enough.

Of Flynn and his unfounded suspicions.

Of the whole darn world.

She straightened her shoulders. "Mr. Donovan, you owe me one hell of an apology," she said, determined to stand up to him and to keep on standing up to him for as long as it took.

One of his arrogant brows lifted. "For what?"

"You're wrong about me."

"I don't think so." His eyes were so cold that not even the hot Darwin sun could defrost them. "Now, stop wasting my time." He picked up the car keys and held them out to her. "Take it or leave it."

She looked at the keys, then back at his derisive face. "Thanks. I'll pass."

"Danielle…" he growled.

All at once she knew that if she didn't get out of there she was going to burst into tears. She twirled toward the door.

"Where are you going?" he demanded.

Moisture welled in her eyes and she tried to blink it away. "That's not your concern."

"Danielle, stop," he warned.

She kept on walking out the door and hurried toward the elevator.

"Danielle, I mean it," he said, coming up behind her.

"Big deal," she choked as she punched the button for the elevator and the doors slid open. Thankfully it was vacant and she rushed into it before she did something really stupid, like crying.

But she only managed to hold back the tears until she stepped inside, half-blindly pressing the ground floor button. Then they swelled up in her eyes so quickly she couldn't even see what she was doing.

All at once Flynn stormed in next to her, making her jump. She turned her back and blinked rapidly, determined not to let him see how upset she was. This would just be another thing for him to accuse her of faking.

She heard the elevator door close.

A moment passed.

"Danielle, look at me," he said softly.

"No." She didn't want him to see her like this. Not when she felt like a weepy female.

His hand touched her shoulder and he gently turned her around. At the oddly concerned gleam in his eyes, she moaned and did the exact opposite of what she'd told herself not to do. She burst into tears.

After a moment or two a snarling sound came from deep in his throat and he pulled her into his arms. "Shh. Don't cry."

"I can't help it," she mumbled into his shirt, hating him, wanting him. Oh, she didn't know what she felt for him.

He gave her his handkerchief and she cried even harder, until she thought she was never going to stop. Until the tears began to dry up and she could sniff for a few more moments. And then she began to notice how wonderful Flynn smelled, the tantalizing warmth of his male body mixing with the clean scent of his shirt.

"Danielle?"

She heard the deep rumble of her name, felt the rapid beat of his heart against her cheek and couldn't seem to pull away. She felt lethargic all of a sudden. Wonderfully lethargic. Heat was engulfing her. Male heat. And it was coming from Flynn. She had the sudden urge to take long, intimate breaths.

"Danielle?"

This time she did move back. And looked up into dark eyes that made her heart skip a beat. Up close like this, the look was much more than powerful. It was potent. And possessive. She dared not breath. Otherwise he would kiss her. Would lay his lips upon hers and ravish her mouth, and she didn't think she would be able to resist him.

He bent his head….

The elevator jolted to a stop, making her jump back, horrified by what she'd been about to let him do to her.

He reached out to steady her as she bumped against the wall. "Careful," he said roughly, his touch making her skin quiver, as if the thin material of her top beneath his hands didn't exist.

She took a shaky breath. It was time to put some distance between them. "I think I need eyes in the back of my head," she said, trying to sound glib but the huskiness in her voice gave her away.

"It would help," he muttered, a vein throbbing at his temple, telling her he was as affected as she was. "Maybe then I wouldn't want you."

She gave a soft gasp. "I—"

"Don't say a word, Danielle. Not a word or I'll carry you back up to my office and make love to you right now."

She'd known there was a sexual spark between them from the start, but hearing him say out loud that he still wanted her was shocking. "But…I'm pregnant."

"I know," he said, his mouth grim.

For a moment she stood there, stunned as the doors behind him slid open to an empty lobby. Flynn Donovan still wanted her. And dear God, she wanted him, too. But pregnant widows weren't supposed to want a man. It just wasn't done.

Yet how could she want a man who thought the worst of her? A man who had accused her of stealing his money? Of lying and cheating?

A moment crept by, then with a hint of regret in his eyes, he took her arm, gently pulled her past him and pushed her out into the lobby, but not before she felt his hard body brush against her own.

"The car's yours," he said roughly, not moving from the elevator. His eyes held hers for another instant, tiny flames firing in them, then anger flared and he reached out and shoved the car keys in her hand. "Take them." He turned and stabbed the elevator button.

The door closed shut between them and she took a steadying breath. Flynn Donovan stirred a need within her that was more than physical. Something deeper. More intimate. *Oh, God.* Hadn't she had enough heartache where men were concerned?

It was all his PA's fault that he had to return Danielle's purse after work, Flynn decided. If it were left to him, he would have sent it back by courier. As it was, if *he* didn't do it, she would. She'd said so when he'd returned from seeing Danielle off at the elevator and Connie had stood there with the purse in hand and a worried look in her eyes. He hadn't been about to let that happen. If Danielle got her clutches into Connie, then she would have won.

Of course, his PA was more than happy for him to return the purse. Delighted in fact. He was still in her good books after yesterday when he'd walked into the office and ordered her to go buy a new car.

"For you?" Connie had said with a frown.

"For Danielle Ford," he'd snapped.

Her eyes had widened. "What about the loan?"

"She refused to tear it up."

Connie had nodded, as if agreeing. "She has integrity, that one."

He'd shaken his head, still amazed his usually perceptive assistant couldn't see the truth. "She's just trying to pull the wool over your eyes."

"I don't know why."

He did, but he'd refused to mention his theory that Danielle was after a rich man to marry her. How else could she keep herself and her baby in the manner to which she was accustomed?

"No matter. Right now a car is her immediate concern. That's if it meets with your approval," he'd derided.

Her eyes had softened with understanding. "That isn't why you did it, but thank you, Flynn."

"Connie, don't turn me into a saint."

"Heaven forbid," she'd joked. Then her forehead had creased. "Hmm. Perhaps I should go and see—"

"No," he'd growled.

"But someone should keep an eye on her."

"Don't get involved, Connie."

"But—"

"Say one more thing about Danielle Ford and I'll fire you myself." And he'd meant it.

She'd given him a look that said it wasn't over, but she'd done what he'd ordered and bought a car.

So now he would return the purse, then go home and dress for his date and he'd make damn sure he enjoyed himself tonight, he decided, as he strode down the hallway toward Danielle's penthouse door. He had a date with an ex-lover and he fully intended to make the most of his night and the last thing he needed was a glimpse of Danielle Ford to remind him what he couldn't have with her.

His eyes narrowed when he saw her door standing open. Bloody hell, was she *expecting* him? Had she deliberately left the purse on his desk? Of course she must have.

Anger filled him as he strode forward, the sound of the television meeting his ears as he got closer to the open doorway. "Danielle?" he called out in a sharp tone.

No answer.

He stepped into the living room and called louder, "Danielle?"

Still no answer.

He looked around the room and over to the kitchen. Why didn't she answer?

A muffled sound came from the other direction and a frisson of fear rolled down his spine. Despite it, he strode forward, a knot growing in his gut with each step he took. If she'd hurt herself...

He pushed the door open. And there she was, wrapping her hair up in a towel, having just stepped out of the shower. She looked up at the doorway and screamed.

Then she let out a shaky breath. "Oh, Flynn. It's only you."

Only him.

His eyes dropped from her face to her breasts, over her still-flat stomach to the blond triangle of hair at the junction of her thighs. His body hardened in the hot, steamy room. This woman would turn up any man's blood pressure. She was a seductress. A sexy witch. And he wanted her more than he'd ever wanted a woman before.

"Flynn?"

The soft sound of his name on her lips made him want to take her in his arms. To press her breasts against his chest. To ease the ache between her thighs, *their* thighs, with the sweetest possession of all.

His gaze roved back up to her face, and her eyes told him what he already knew. Danielle Ford wanted him as much as he wanted her.

"You're beautiful," he rasped and saw her eyes deepen to a smoky blue.

"I'm—" Apprehension flicked across her face. Suddenly she made a grab for the short robe resting on the towel rack. "Pregnant," she said unsteadily, sliding her arms into the material and pulling it close. "I think you've forgotten that."

"You're still sexy, Danielle. Incredibly so."

"Don't," she whispered.

"Don't what?"

"Come in here and seduce me."

He noted the way the soft, sky-blue material of her robe clung to her damp breasts. "That's funny. I thought you were the one doing the seducing."

Color flooded her face. "How? By stepping out of my own shower?"

He straightened. "Your door was open," he reminded her, then held up the purse. "And you left this in my office today."

Recognition flickered in her eyes. "Oh. Yes, I know. I was going to come by and get it tomorrow."

He sent her a mocking look.

Her eyes widened. "You think I left it there deliberately?"

"You mean you didn't?"

She opened her mouth to speak, then closed it, her forehead crinkling. "Wait a minute. What do you mean my door was open? It was closed. I'm sure it was. I always close it."

"Perhaps the lock's faulty?" he said, sneering, knowing she'd set him up well and truly.

She stiffened. "Perhaps it is. The Realtor said they'd changed the locks." She jerkily pulled the towel from her head and combed her fingers through her hair, then stopped to look at him. "Anyway, I'd appreciate it if you'd leave."

He wasn't used to being dismissed, certainly not by the woman he wanted. "Found another willing male to help you out?" he said cynically.

She bristled with indignation. "I resent that remark. I've never once asked for your help. You forced the car on me. I didn't want to take it, remember?"

"You needed help for your baby."

"We would have survived without it."

"No doubt." This woman was a survivor of the worst kind. She survived on other people's money.

"You don't seem to understand that my independence is important to me," she said, the proud tilt of her head at odds with what he knew about her.

"Don't I?"

She drew herself up as she tightened her robe. "In the future I'll thank you to stay away from me. I accepted the car but that doesn't give you the right to walk into my apartment anytime you like."

His mouth pressed into a grim line. "That isn't why I'm here," he pointed out.

"Sure it isn't," she mocked, trying to turn the tables on him, looking so darn beautiful that she grabbed his breath away. If he didn't get out of here soon he was going to march up to her, pull her into his arms and kiss her until she surrendered to him completely.

Drawing a sharp breath, he twisted on his heels and headed toward the front door. The woman was a danger to herself and to every man she smiled at. Even the ones she didn't smile at would succumb to her beauty. All men were suckers for a beautiful lady with charisma.

"I'd better check that lock," he said roughly, not believing that it was faulty but needing to make sure.

"There's no need," she said quickly, coming up

behind him. "The landlord will fix it if there's a problem."

He stopped dead, and so did she. "I thought you'd want to fix it yourself," he scoffed. "Seeing you're so independent and all."

Her enticing lips tightened. "You're taking that out of context."

He didn't think so. "Anyway, if it *is* faulty—" and his tone said he very much doubted it "—you won't get the landlord to look at it before Monday. And I don't want to get up tomorrow morning and find your murder front-page news."

"Don't be silly," she scoffed, but all at once her voice sounded uncertain as she touched her stomach.

A shiver went down his spine again. "I'm checking the lock whether you like it or not." He strode to the door.

Unfortunately it didn't take him long to spot a problem with the catch. He swore, not liking the sudden feeling of guilt. And not liking that perhaps he had been wrong about her.

This time.

"What is it?" she said behind him.

"Looks like I owe you an apology."

She expelled a little sigh. "See. I told you I was telling the truth." She moved closer. "What's wrong with it?"

The exotic fragrance she'd rubbed all over her body was suddenly blinding him to all the reasons he should step back and leave this apartment before it was too late. "It isn't catching properly."

"Where?" she said, moving even closer.

And that was it.

All at once the air hummed with electricity. As if she felt it, she turned to face him. Their eyes met and she gave a soft gasp, and in that heartbeat, Flynn knew he had to kiss her or regret it for the rest of his life.

"Don't stop me, Danielle," he growled and didn't give her time to argue. He lowered his head, his eyes homing in on her mouth. For a moment she held out against him and he knew she was fighting herself rather than him. Then her lips quivered and opened on the smallest sigh of surrender.

Adrenaline pumped into him and his tongue slipped inside her to taste the moist, dark warmth of her. She tasted superb. Just as he'd expected. Just as he'd imagined since the first time he'd seen her.

Without warning, her arms inched up and slid around his neck, pulling him closer. He could feel her against him, arousing him, and suddenly everything was getting out of control. *His* control. She was pregnant, for God's sake. He had to stop.

He broke off the kiss and swore, "Hell."

"Flynn?" she whispered, her eyes darkened with that smoky hue again.

Heat engulfed him and he groaned. "Just one more kiss," he muttered, pulling her to him.

A goodbye kiss.

A farewell kiss.

A kiss to end all kisses.

Only, when their lips met for a second time, it suddenly didn't matter that she was pregnant. Nor that she was a woman out to get all that she could. Nothing mattered except the delicious taste of her, the glorious scent of her, the explosive feel of her in his arms, rubbing up against him, turning him on.

Shuddering, he let his mouth slide along her cheek to her ear, catching her delicate earlobe between his lips, then his teeth, laving it with his tongue.

"Flynn, we have to stop." She moaned with pleasure, inflaming him further.

He pushed some wet strands of her hair aside with his lips and trailed kisses down the column of her throat, pressing his mouth against her wildly beating pulse. "Must we?" He just needed to touch her some more. Maybe then he'd get enough of her.

"We…have to." Her husky tones told him she had her eyes closed, savoring each precious moment. He did the same as he inhaled against her collarbone. Her scent was driving him wild.

"Let me love you just a little," he murmured, deciding to damn the consequences just for a moment more and moved back to push the silky robe off her shoulders, exposing the tips of her nipples. He looked down at her full breasts and sucked in air. "Beautiful. They're made for a man's hands. *My* hands."

She lifted heavy eyelids. "Yes."

"And for my tongue."

"Oh, yes!"

He slid the material off her shoulders, fully exposing her in a way that highlighted each golden globe. An aching need hit him right in the gut, then lower to where his erection strained against his trousers.

He ran a finger from one nipple to the other, her silky soft skin puckering to his touch as she rested her head back against the wall, giving short little puffs of breath. He repeated the action.

Then he ran his thumbs across each brown peak, before squeezing those little pebbles between his fingers. She moaned and her eyes feathered shut, and something deep inside him abated, filling him with a sense of rightness. He was meant to be here, with her in his arms. Right now, in this moment of time.

Groaning, he bent his head and took a nipple in his mouth, flicking it with his tongue.

"Flynn," she sobbed in a guttural sound that seemed to come from deep within her.

He did it again, then began to suck, harder and harder, wanting to give her more and more. He could hear the pounding of his heart in his ears, telling him to give her everything she needed. That only *he* could give it to her.

She moved restlessly and a picture of those blond womanly curls came to mind, making his fingers itch to touch her there. Lord knew he wanted to find out what she felt like.

He kissed her again and slowly slid his palm over her stomach, then down to the essence of the woman. God, she was wet and warm against his fingers.

He kissed her deeply, moving his fingers against her soft nub, stroking once, stroking twice. He wanted to give her pleasure. No, he wanted to give her a pleasure like she'd never known before.

"Let yourself go," he murmured against the corner of her mouth and touched her some more.

At first there was a slight ripple through her body, then her legs began to quiver. She gripped his shoulders, panting heavily, head flung back, eyes closed.

"That's it, sweetheart." He relished the expressive emotions flittering across her face as she reached closer to fulfillment.

And then the tremors of arousal began and she cried out his name as she went up in flames. She shattered as his fingers slicked back and forth. If he'd been inside her, he would have felt her grip and release as she rode the waves of ecstasy. It was almost enough to send a man over the edge.

He held her until the turbulence inside her slowed to a halt. She leaned against him, resting her head on his shoulder while she caught her breath.

Finally she looked up at him and in her eyes was pure embarrassment. She looked more than beautiful. Stunning. Intense male possessiveness ripped through him, even as he wondered about her self-consciousness.

"Flynn, I—"

"Don't say anything." He gathered the sides of her robe together and tied it with the sash.

She licked her slightly swollen lips. "But you haven't… You didn't…"

"No, and I don't need to," he rasped.

"But—"

"No buts, Danielle." He gazed at her, forcing himself to concentrate on the moment. "I enjoyed watching you."

She gave a soft gasp and he bent his head, quickly taking advantage of her open mouth. He parted her lips with his tongue, then spent a long moment absorbing the heady taste of her. It was a taste flavored by a new sensuousness between them.

Then suddenly there was a knock on the door.

Danielle broke off the kiss, pushed at his chest. "Oh, God!" she gasped.

He frowned as the outside world intruded. "What's the matter?"

"It's Monica," she whispered, her eyes darting down the hallway as if looking for an escape.

"Monica?"

She glanced back at him. "Um…my mother-in-law," she said, then looked away nervously, giving him the impression she didn't want him to know too much about the other woman.

His jaw clenched at the reminder that Danielle had been married. That she'd belonged to another man. Robert would have touched her, loving her in many ways, making her his own. Flynn was suddenly jealous of the other man. Of every second Robert Ford had spent with her.

"Don't answer," he said roughly, keeping his voice low.

Her eyes clouded over. "I have to. She's coming for dinner. It's my birthday."

Something odd kicked inside him. "Your birthday?"

"Yes," she said almost absentmindedly, then bit her lip nervously. "If I don't answer the door, she'll think I'm still at work and…"

He jolted. So she *did* have a regular job and didn't just volunteer at the hospital as he'd imagined.

"Then if I don't come home, she's likely to call the police."

"Did you say she was your mother-in-law, or your mother?" he mocked, not liking the sound of this Monica.

"Mother-in-law," she mumbled, missing his sarcasm.

"Then just open the door and act as if nothing happened."

And that would be the biggest lie ever.

She moistened her lips, her eyes darting past his shoulder, looking everywhere but at him. "I can't. She wouldn't understand."

The muscles at the back of his neck tightened. "Are you scared of her?"

Her eyes swung back to him. "Of course not," she said, but there was a hollow ring to her words, and he knew she was definitely scared of something. "She's just…" She winced. "Well, she's Robert's mother. I don't want her to find us like this."

"Like what? I was only checking your lock," he drawled.

She blushed, her gaze dropping to his chest. "Flynn, I don't think—"

Another knock at the door cut across her words, making her jump. Flynn swore softly. This was a ridiculous situation.

She brushed back her damp hair, then tightened the collar of her robe. She swallowed. "I have to face her."

He suddenly felt proud of her, so he dropped a light kiss on her lips, tempted to linger. He wanted to say to hell with this Monica, but if he did that, then he'd have to sweep Danielle up in his arms and carry her to the bedroom for a night of hot pleasure.

And then what?

He shuddered. It was as well this Monica would call the police. It was the wake-up call he needed. From this point he would back off and leave Danielle to get on with her life. In about six months time she would become a mother, for God's sake. And he'd never seen anyone sexier.

"Flynn, I'm ready."

He gave a nod, then pulled the door open, making the well-dressed woman on the other side almost leap out of her skin.

"Monica," Danielle exclaimed, pretending surprise, though Flynn didn't think she did a good job of it, considering she was such an accomplished liar at times. "I didn't realize you were there."

The mother-in-law's gaze traveled from one to the other, then up and down, her obsidian eyes turning colder by degrees. "So I see."

"This is Flynn." Danielle gave a smile but he saw the uneasiness beneath. "He's been checking the lock on my door."

"Really?" Monica said haughtily, then dismissed him by smiling coolly. "You should have called, dear. I know a locksmith."

He'd bet a thousand dollars she didn't, Flynn thought, taking an instant dislike to Danielle's mother-in-law, noticing how her smile didn't reach her eyes. She was too cold. And calculating.

"Yes, well," Danielle said. "The landlord will have to fix it now. Flynn hasn't got the right equipment."

"Oh, I don't know about that," he drawled, and

was pleased when two spots of color appeared on Danielle's cheeks.

Monica looked at Flynn. "If only my Robbie were here. He was good at fixing things."

"I'm sure he *was*," Flynn said, emphasizing the last word. If Monica thought she was warning him off Danielle, then she could think again. He'd already made the decision to stay away and it had nothing to do with her mother-in-law.

Monica's narrowed eyes told him she got the message, and right at that moment, Flynn could see how much Robert Ford had been like his mother. From the moment he'd met the other man he'd disliked him intensely.

As if Danielle sensed something going on between the two of them, she turned toward him, her eyes agitated. "Well, thanks again, Flynn," she said, almost pushing him out the door. "I appreciate your help."

He was tempted to stay just to annoy this Monica. Instead he stepped through the doorway and into the hall. "Make sure you get the lock fixed as soon as possible."

"I will. And good night."

"Yes, *goodbye*," Monica said, moving past him into the apartment, almost elbowing him aside. "Nice meeting you."

"And you." He could play the game as well as she could, he mused, watching her continue on to the living room. Her rigid back gave him an immense sense of satisfaction.

Danielle glanced over her shoulder, again reminding him she was uneasy with this woman in her home, and a protective instinct rose in him, which he firmly squashed. He had no doubt Danielle would continue to hold firm against the other woman. After all, Danielle could take care of herself. He had to remember that.

"I'd better go in." Danielle started to close the door, then stopped briefly, awareness in her eyes shooting desire through every region of his body. "Thank you for returning my purse."

He held her gaze for one long moment, angry she was who she was, but wanting her with every fiber of his being. "It was my pleasure," he rasped, watching with satisfaction as a flush spread up her neck to her face just before she closed the door.

He stood there for a moment and inhaled her scent still clinging to him. Then he spun on his heels and headed toward the elevator. He was supposed to be going out tonight but the thought of talking to another woman, of being with another woman, of making love to a woman other than the woman he wanted, filled him with distaste.

Dammit, there was no way he could go on his date now. Not after what he'd just shared with Danielle. He only hoped that even this small sample of how pleasurable it could be with Danielle Ford hadn't ruined his love life.

Forever.

Danielle shut the door, then let out a shaky sigh. She had been so close to disaster just now. If Flynn had mentioned the loan to spite her… If Monica had decided to use it to get the baby…

No, she wouldn't let it happen to her.

Straightening her shoulders, she took a deep breath before turning into the living room to face Monica. Her mother-in-law was bound to say something about Flynn having been in the apartment.

"Here. Let me take those," she said when she saw Monica with a pile of her personal papers in the other woman's hands.

Monica spun around, a flash of guilt crossing her face. "Oh, you startled me. I was just moving them so I could sit down."

Danielle was sure she'd been reading them, not moving them, but she let it pass. They were only some bills and the lease to the apartment, which she'd been meaning to put away, anyway. Thankfully there was nothing about the loan in among that lot, she thought with intense relief as she took the papers and put them in the bureau drawer, out of sight.

Monica sat down on the couch and stabbed her with her eyes. "Tell me, Danielle. How do you know Flynn Donovan?"

Danielle had already prepared herself for the question. "He was visiting my neighbor in the other penthouse," she lied, hating it but knowing it had to be done. "My door was open and he came to tell me and we discovered the lock was faulty."

"So you don't know him personally?" she questioned further.

"No." Something occurred to Danielle. "But obviously you knew who he was."

Monica shrugged. "Only from what I've read in the newspapers."

Surprisingly, Monica appeared to accept the explanation. Then her assessing gaze raked down Danielle's bathrobe. "That's new, isn't it?"

Danielle suddenly felt exposed and vulnerable, even more than when she'd stood naked in front of Flynn, if that was possible.

"Yes, it is," she said, trying not to get defensive. She'd bought the silk robe a couple of weeks ago when she'd needed something to cheer herself up and the price had been so cheap it had almost jumped off the rack at her.

Another look at Monica, and Danielle decided she'd be too uncomfortable to stay dressed like this another minute. "I'll just go and change."

"Hmm." Monica weighed her with a critical squint. "I'm not sure Robbie would like it on you."

That old feeling of being smothered returned and Danielle stiffened. She had to be strong and continue to dodge being snared by her mother-in-law's need to control. "Really?"

"And, Danielle, dear, a bit of advice. You shouldn't wear something like that in front of another man. It may give him ideas, especially one as rich and successful as Flynn Donovan."

Danielle whirled around and started walking to her bedroom so Monica wouldn't see her face turning red. "Not in my condition it wouldn't."

"You'd be surprised. Some men find pregnancy rather attractive," Monica warned, her voice rising as Danielle continued walking.

"I'm sure you're wrong," Danielle said, then closed her bedroom door and leaned back against it.

Heat washed over her body and her legs trembled. From the moment Flynn had stepped into her bathroom, she'd been his for the taking. Oh, she'd fought herself all the way to the front door, but when she'd turned and seen the hot desire in his eyes, she had melted for him.

But it had been so long since she'd felt attraction for a man. So long since she'd made love to a man she desired. Flynn had made her come alive again, had recognized her needs and taken her beyond the edge of satisfaction. She'd never had such an experience before. He made her feel like a woman again. And he'd given back what had slowly diminished in her marriage to Robert. Her sense of feminine self.

For that she owed Flynn Donovan a lot.

Of course, that didn't make him any less arrogant, nor the right man for her, she reminded herself. She needed to keep that in mind and fend off her attraction for him.

Just then, there was a light knock on the door. "Are you coming out, Danielle? I want to give you your birthday present."

Danielle let out a slow breath and counted to ten. Monica always did this, stalking her until she felt smothered. Robert had been the same. And that was a timely reminder that the battle for independence had been too hard fought and won.

"I'll be there in a minute, Monica. Why don't you put the coffee on?"

A moment's silence, then she said, "Fine."

Danielle waited a moment more, then pushed herself

away from the door with trembling hands. She was never going to let herself be dictated to again.

Never.

And that applied to Flynn Donovan.

No matter how wonderful he made her feel.

Five

After the function, Flynn dropped his date off at her apartment, drove home to his mansion in Cullen Bay, then spent the early hours of the morning sitting on the balcony of his master bedroom. An electrical storm had raged during the evening while he'd been at the dinner, and now his lushly landscaped garden was beautifully moonlit.

He'd realized one thing tonight. He'd rather spend an evening being antagonized by Danielle than being sweet talked by a bevy of beautiful women.

God, what *was* it about Danielle Ford he couldn't shake? As much as a part of him didn't want to see this woman who was far from an angel, he knew his body still hungered after her. It was a hunger that he wasn't about to appease, so why was he putting himself through this? He couldn't have her…shouldn't have her…but he'd tormented himself anyway.

Yet every time he looked into her blue eyes it weakened his determination to stay away from her. And tonight…no, yesterday…he couldn't stop thinking about the way she'd melted for him back there in her apartment.

And that baffled him. For a woman who would have used her body many times to get what she wanted, according to her former husband, she hadn't been as experienced as he'd expected. Her slight hesitation and occasional lack of control…while thoroughly tantalizing…had told him otherwise.

Dammit, she just didn't add up. She seemed to be a mixture of truth and lies. Of innocence and guilt. Independent yet reliant. Look at the way she'd left her door open for him…or not. The lock *had* been faulty, he admitted.

And she'd mentioned her job in the stress of the moment. So it was a real job, after all, not a volunteer one as he'd suspected. It was time he actually got that report done on her. A personal one this time, not just a financial one. He wanted to know everything about her. Everything and more from the day she'd been born.

And dammit, yesterday had been her birthday and he hadn't known until too late. It turned out that the car he'd given her had been an inadvertently well-timed gift, but spending the evening with a cold, unfeeling mother-in-law who obviously didn't have an unselfish bone in her body wasn't exactly a great way to celebrate.

Danielle deserved better.

She also deserved an Oscar, he forced himself to remember as he hopped in his Mercedes just after breakfast, intending to drive to her apartment before she went to work. He was determined to make sure she had dinner with him tonight.

Him and no other man.

He was just leaving his driveway, about to turn out onto the main road when a figure stepped in front of the car. He swore as he slammed on the brakes, stopping just short of hitting the person.

Then he saw who it was.

Monica Ford.

His jaw clenched as he got out of his car and walked toward her. She'd obviously been waiting for him to leave his house, though how she'd known where he lived made him uneasy. He didn't like this woman.

And that hated look in her eyes said she was still remembering meeting him yesterday at Danielle's apartment.

"Monica," he said, inclining his head in greeting.

"It's Mrs. Ford to you, Mr. Donovan," she spat.

He paused for effect. "I see."

"Do you?"

She was obviously spoiling for a fight.

"Why are you here?"

She glared at him. "I want you to stay away from Danielle. Or you'll be sorry."

He felt his anger rise in response. "I don't take kindly to threats."

"Danielle and the baby belong to Robert. I won't let you have either of them."

Sudden apprehension rolled over in his chest. "Is this some kind of joke?"

She pulled herself up straighter. "My son is no joke. Danielle loves him and he loves her."

He mentally took a step back. "Your son is dead," he pointed out, trying to judge if this woman was as mad as she made out to be.

"How dare you say that!"

He scowled. Whether she was mad or not, she was definitely mentally unbalanced. "Listen, I think you need help."

She wagged a finger at him and hissed, "You just stay out of the picture. That's all the help we want."

We?

Giving him a hateful look, she said, "Whatever you think you're going to get from Danielle won't happen. *I* won't let it." Then she spun on her heels and hurried toward a car parked down the road.

Flynn waited until she'd driven off, a horrible feeling in his gut. She was definitely sick in the head, exactly how sick was the question. But he knew one thing. He preferred her coldness yesterday over the hate today.

He still felt uneasy on the way over to Danielle's place, but more for her sake than his own. He could handle the likes of Monica, but the woman was unstable and he wasn't sure Danielle knew that. He vowed to keep an eye on things though he suspected Monica wouldn't hurt Danielle and the baby. If anything, it was *him* Monica would want to hurt.

When Danielle opened her front door, he pushed all that to the back of his mind.

Adrenaline surged through him at the sight of her. He

hadn't seen her since last evening…since she'd come apart in his hands.

She was as sexy as hell. Her coral halter-necked top doing marvelous things for her skin tone and denim shorts showing off those gorgeous legs of hers, down to her bare feet.

She lifted her chin in the air. "Flynn, we need to talk," she said, not inviting him in, obviously ready to do battle. "I don't want you getting the wrong idea about last night. About it leading anywhere or anything. I mean…" All at once she faltered a little in her speech. "We're both adults and things got out of hand, that's all."

"In more ways than one," he drawled, her reluctance to have anything to do with him stirring his senses and urging him to take her in his arms and force her to change her mind.

"Last night was a mistake. I'm not ready for an affair. I'm having a baby."

His mouth flattened into a straight line as her words hit home. He may not be able to argue with the truth, but one thing was for certain. If she hadn't been pregnant, she'd be in his bed right now and they wouldn't be merely *talking* about making love. He'd be inside her warm body, knowing this woman intimately.

Just thinking about it aroused him more than he'd ever been before. And it had nothing to do with being celibate for a couple of months now. It was all to do with Danielle.

His jaw clenched. "Did you phone the landlord about getting your lock fixed?"

She blinked, took a moment to note the change of

subject, then gave a nod. "Someone will be here Monday."

Pleasure coursed through him that she had followed his instructions, in this at least. "Make sure you close your door properly until then," he said, partly thinking of Monica.

Danielle held herself stiffly, a rush of heat coming into her cheeks. "Why are you here, Flynn?"

He had to think past how gorgeous she looked with that soft color tingeing her high cheekbones. "I didn't get to say happy birthday to you last night."

Her eyes widened in surprise, then mellowed with something that hinted at gratitude. But in the blink of an eye, they suddenly hardened. "What's the catch?"

"No catch."

"You could have sent flowers."

"But then," he drawled, "I wouldn't have had the chance to blackmail you into having dinner with me tonight."

Her hand slipped from the doorknob. "Wh-what?"

"I'll pick you up at seven." He started to walk away.

"Wait!"

Something in her tone made him stop and turn back to face her. A vulnerable look in her eyes made his chest tighten.

"Flynn, I—" she hesitated "—I don't think we should."

An unusual feeling of tenderness rose up inside him but he firmly squashed it. "Danielle, you owe me."

Her chin angled higher. "I've told you. I'm paying back the money for the loan and the car."

"I'm talking about the lock."

She looked confused. "But you didn't fix it."

"No, but I came close," he said, pleased at the double entendre.

Her cheeks reddened. "I know you've been more than generous but I think I'll stay home tonight."

"Alone?" he said sharply as jealousy slithered through him. And that was happening far too often for his liking. No other woman had ever made him feel that particular emotion before. He wasn't going to let it get a stranglehold now.

"Yes."

"Seven," he ordered, turning toward the elevator so she couldn't see his intense relief. "Be ready."

He didn't wait for her to answer. As if on cue, the doors opened for him and he stepped inside.

Danielle then spent the day warring between feeling angry with Flynn for his "Me Tarzan, you Jane" attitude, but suspecting he had a kind heart beneath all that arrogance. Certainly Robert had only ever taken her out to dinner once on her birthday and that had been when they were courting. After their marriage, he and Monica had mostly preferred to dine at home on special occasions.

It was this very reminder of the past that made Danielle change her mind about going out with Flynn tonight. She was a free woman and she would do as she liked and go out with whomever she liked. Just because it happened to be Flynn Donovan…

When her doorbell rang at seven, she nervously patted some wisps of blond hair back into her chignon, then smoothed the front of her short black dress. The soft silky material was complemented by a loose-fitting jacket of the same material.

She swung open the door and her breath caught in her throat. Flynn looked incredibly handsome in a black suit that emphasized the width of his shoulders and the length of his legs. A white shirt beneath his jacket only added to his compelling sense of presence.

"You are more beautiful each time I see you," he murmured, his voice deep and husky, a light at the back of his eyes hinting that just looking at her switched on something inside him.

She wished she could have stayed angry with him. It would have given her the impetus to ignore the admiration he made no effort to hide. Instead, she dissolved like bubbles in a bath.

"Thank you," she whispered, then cleared her throat, finding her mental balance. "I didn't know how fancy this restaurant is, so I wasn't sure what to wear."

"You're perfect."

Her heart skipped a beat but didn't settle to a nice easy pace. "Um...I'll get my purse." She turned and walked over to the sofa, breathing easier as she put some distance between them. But when she turned back, Flynn had entered the apartment, closing the door behind him.

"This is for you," he said, holding a small gift-wrapped box in his hands she hadn't noticed before.

"It is?" Silly delight skipped along her spine before she brought herself back down to earth. He'd already helped her too much. Okay, so he was wealthy and could afford it, but taking her to dinner was more than enough.

"I'm sorry. I can't accept another present from you, Flynn. I hardly know you," she said, reminding him they were nothing to each other, when all was said and done.

"But you *do* know me, Danielle. I was the man who made you crumble in my hands yesterday." He jerked his hand behind him. "By that very door."

The breath hitched in her throat but she managed one word. "Flynn."

"Remember?"

How could she forget the way he'd made her feel? How his touch had scorched her body. How he'd taken her to the heights, then released her into a tide of passion.

"Yes, I remember." She wet her suddenly dry lips. "Nevertheless, I—"

"You haven't even seen it yet," he pointed out dryly, moving toward her.

"No, but—"

"It isn't jewelry, if that's what's bothering you."

They both knew that wasn't really what bothered her. It was the attraction between them. The sensual tension that threatened to spiral out of control every time they were together.

He stopped right in front of her. She could smell his aftershave, a distinct scent of sandalwood and cedar that endorsed his masculinity and threatened to overwhelm her.

Feeling it would be churlish to refuse now, she shakily held out her evening purse. "Hold this please," she said, accepting the small box from him. The quicker she got this over with the better. And, yes, she really was a little excited to be getting a present.

She ripped the paper slightly as she undid the package to reveal a bottle of an expensive perfume she'd wanted to buy herself for ages but hadn't. This particular scent was way out of her price range these days, and when she could have afforded it—when she'd been married—she hadn't wanted to wear it. Not for Robert.

"Oh, my."

"You don't like it?"

Her eyes shone. "Of course I do. I love it."

"*Allure,*" he murmured. "I think the name's appropriate, don't you?"

A quiver surged through her veins. "Thank you," she said, deciding to ignore the remark. "It's just what I wanted." About to place the box down on the sofa, she froze as he reached out and touched her arm. Without warning, a billow of awareness fell over the room.

"And this is what *I* want," he drawled, putting his hand under her chin, tilting her mouth up to him.

It happened so suddenly she didn't have time to react the way she knew she should. Instead, she trembled as his head lowered toward her. Trembled, but her lips parted even before their mouths touched.

It was a stunning kiss, one that swept her straight back to yesterday, to being in his arms, him doing delicious things to her, doing them with just his mouth this time, nothing else. Nothing but his tongue sliding over hers, his velvet touch so very sensitive against her own. So sensitive that her senses reeled.

She moaned but he continued to caress the moist cavern of her mouth, gentle yet demanding, coaxing her toward abandonment, toward the sensual heaven he offered.

And then, ever so slowly, he began to ease back. He teased her lower lip with his teeth for a long moment, letting the air move in where before there was only him.

Finally his head lifted. He stared into her eyes, his own dark and sensual. "Happy birthday for yesterday, Danielle," he murmured.

"I…" She swallowed, licked her lips, tasted him there. "Um…thank you."

Giving her a look that said he wasn't unaffected, either, he took the package out of her hands and replaced it with her purse. "Let's get out of here," he growled. "Before I kiss you again."

She let him lead her to the door, the touch of his hand searing through the material of her sleeve, the scent of him making her light-headed as they rode down the elevator.

Without speaking they walked out the building toward his parked car. She tried to clear her mind of him but it was impossible with his presence beside her.

It was no better in the confines of his Mercedes. He was so close, almost touching, he only had to lean toward her, pull her toward him.

She swallowed. If it didn't smack of cowardice, she would have hopped out right then and there, thanked him for the offer and gone home. An evening spent watching television was better than feeling so… Well, it was better than *feeling*. Period.

Flynn caught her sneaking a look at him and braked. "It was just a kiss," he rasped.

Her throat felt dry. "I know."

"Then don't look at me like that."

"Like what?" she said, despite herself, despite knowing what he'd say.

"Like you think I'm going to devour you at any moment."

Devour? Yes, he was like a tiger circling her, ready to leap and make love to her at the first hint of weakness. If she ever let him past her guard, she'd pay for it dearly.

His sensuous lips began to twitch. "I promise you I only pounce when there's a full moon. And there's no full moon tonight."

The absurdity of it made her smile to herself. "I'm glad to hear it."

"Relax, Danielle."

She arched an elegant brow. "Now that *is* asking too much," she mocked, and received a stunningly sexy smile in return.

Fortunately for her, he pulled out of the parking spot and they drove the few kilometers along the waterfront in a less tense atmosphere. The amazing orange of the sky as the sun started to sink below the horizon calmed her and made her feel as if she might just be able to get through this evening.

Situated on the esplanade, the restaurant was fashionably busy. The maître d' welcomed Flynn with reverence and immediately escorted them to an intimate table for two in the corner with a spectacular view of the now dark, turquoise ocean beaded by the last rays of the setting sun.

But she couldn't look out the window forever, and eventually turned back to the beauty of her immediate surroundings. Leafy ferns near their table provided a sense of privacy she could have done without as she glanced around the elegant decor, honing in on the small dance floor at one end of the room. Her skin quivered at the thought of dancing in Flynn's arms, but perhaps she was getting ahead of herself. Perhaps he didn't dance.

And perhaps the world had just stopped turning. There was no way he wouldn't take the opportunity to get her in his arms again. She knew that as surely as *sexual appetite* was his middle name.

"They seem to know you here," she said for something to say after the waiter took their order for drinks.

"I've been here once or twice."

With who? she almost asked, then decided it was none of her business whom he took to dinner.

Right then, a tall, extremely handsome and well-dressed man around Flynn's age spied them from across the room and came striding toward them.

"Flynn, I *thought* that was you," he said with a smile that said he was really pleased to see him.

"Damien," Flynn said, surprising Danielle when his face relaxed into a smile, surprising her even more when he stood up and the two men gave each other a brief hug.

Flynn pulled back. "What are you doing here? I thought you were in Rome this week."

"I was, but I had to come back for a series of meetings in Sydney." Damien glanced at Danielle and gave her the full impact of his shrewd, knowing eyes. "Hi, I'm Damien Trent," he said, holding out his hand. "And I'll be taking my last breath before my friend bothers to introduce us."

She put her hand in his and gave a polite smile. "I'm Danielle Ford."

"It's nice to meet you," he said, those eyes studying her in a fashion that reminded her of the man standing next to him.

Goodness, here was another ladykiller, she mused.

Damien looked back at his friend. "I've been meaning to arrange a poker night for when Brant gets back from his honeymoon."

Flynn gave a wry smile, though Danielle sensed he'd noted Damien's scrutiny of her. "I doubt he'll want to play poker for a while yet."

Damien grimaced in good humor. "Don't tell me that. I'll be shattered if Kia doesn't let him come out to play once in a while."

Flynn laughed. "Yeah, I'm sure he'd rather play poker with us than spend time with his new wife."

"You have a point. Kia's a beauty. A man would have to be crazy to leave her side for even a minute." He glanced over his shoulder at the woman at his table. "And speaking of leaving a beauty alone, my date's looking impatient."

"Anyone we know?" Flynn mocked with what was obviously an in-joke.

Damien gave a low chuckle. "No." He held out his

hand for Flynn to shake. "Look, I must run. We've got tickets for a show. I'll give you a call next week about the poker game." He inclined his head at Danielle. "Nice meeting you, Danielle," he said, then strode back over to the other side of the restaurant where the blonde sat at a table waiting for him.

Danielle watched the man walk away, then glanced at Flynn. "He seems like a good friend of yours."

Flynn sat back down, his smile disappearing as an invisible barrier came back up. "Yes, he is."

And that was all he said.

Just then the waiter brought their drinks over, a mineral water for her and a whiskey for Flynn.

Once they were alone again, Flynn picked up his glass, the material of his suit making a soft, sensual sound as he raised his hand in a toast. "Happy birthday for yesterday, Danielle."

She raised her glass and clinked it against his, the small action somehow more intimate than it should be. "Thank you," she said, avoiding his gaze as she took a sip then quickly set the glass down on the table, almost as if it burned her.

She thought of something to say. Something that didn't hint at touching each other. "I gather that was Brant Matthews you two were speaking about?"

He gave her a dry look. "What do I get for telling you the answer?"

"A pleasant evening," she quipped.

"And if I don't tell you?"

"A pleasant evening by yourself."

He gave a soft chuckle that rippled along her spine.

"Then I'd better answer. I don't want to give you any excuse to leave." He leaned back in his chair and took a mouthful of his drink before speaking. "Yes, it was. Brant, Damien and I grew up together."

She'd read about Brant Matthews in the newspapers, so she knew he and Flynn were millionaires. And Damien looked just as successful.

"Was that here in Darwin?"

"Yes. In the same street actually, though the area's a bit more upmarket now than when we were kids," he said with dry humor.

"Do you still have family here?" She found it odd thinking of him with parents and perhaps brothers and sisters. He seemed such a loner at times.

"My parents are dead."

"Oh. I'm sorry." Despite his toneless response, she knew the loss he must feel without them in his life.

He shrugged. "It was a long time ago. My mother died when I was young and my father eventually drank himself to death," he said with a grim twist of his lips.

Her heart cramped with sympathy for him. He wouldn't want her pity but she couldn't help herself. "That's so sad."

"I survived." His look said he was what he was today because of his past, and he'd make no apologies for that. "Now tell me your life story."

She let out a slow breath. He gave an inch but wanted a mile out of her. "My parents are dead, too. They both drowned at the beach when I was thirteen," she said quietly. "We used to live in this little town on the Sunshine Coast in Queensland, until my mother got swept out to sea by a rip and my father tried to save her."

His mouth flattened in a grim line. "Life stinks at times," he said tersely.

"Yes, it does," she said, feeling that same old tightening in her chest whenever she thought of them. "After it happened, I felt like I'd never laugh again. But life goes on. I moved in with an elderly aunt here in Darwin. She treated me like a daughter but she died a few years later. I decided to stay anyway. I had nothing to go back for."

He studied her. "You were young to be on your own."

"I survived," she said, mocking his own words.

Only, he didn't smile as intended. His gaze continued to search her face. She could feel him trying to look inside her mind, her heart, her soul. She tried to break away from that mesmerizing look but couldn't.

Thankfully the waiter returned with the menu and she was able to look away and take a breath. Flynn ordered swordfish steak without reading the menu but she spent the next few minutes deciding on a seafood cocktail entrée, followed by Tasmanian grilled salmon. Through it all, she could still feel him watching her, assessing her through her past.

"How long were you married?" he suddenly demanded, once the waiter departed.

She took a sip of her drink before answering. "Three years."

"Were you happy?"

Her hand gripped her glass tighter. "No." Those years

had almost choked the life out of her. Of course, he wouldn't understand that. As far as he was concerned, she and Robert deserved each other.

He frowned. "No?"

"I guess that's not entirely true. The first year Robert and I were quite happy."

A nerve pulsed near his temple. "So what happened?"

She expelled a shaky breath. "I just don't know. One minute we were in love and the next…it was gone." She grimaced. "Perhaps if Robert and I had lived alone it would've been different. But with Monica there, as well—"

"Monica *lived* with you?" he said, his eyebrows shooting upward.

"Yes. Robert didn't want to leave her on her own, and I could understand that. Her husband died years ago. Until I came along it was only her and Robert."

One corner of his mouth twisted. "Her husband's probably not dead. He's hiding."

She gave a delicate snort. "Don't I know how that feels."

He watched her with a measuring look. "You got out, that's the main thing. It would have taken courage standing up to someone like Monica."

She blinked rapidly even as a lump welled in her throat. He was admitting that he understood about Monica, at least, and that touched her deeply.

"Thank you," she murmured. "It did take courage."

He considered her across the table. "I gather this is the basis for your stand on independence?"

She inclined her head. "Yes. Having someone like Monica around really made me appreciate living alone."

And Robert had been his mother's son.

"Does she frighten you?"

She paused. "You asked me that last night, too, and I said no."

"Are you sure that's the truth?"

She tilted her head with a frown. "Why are you pushing?"

He shrugged. "No reason."

"Tell me about your job," he suddenly said.

She hesitated, confused by all the questions. "Er… what do you want to know?"

"You said yesterday Monica expected you to be home from work in time for her arrival. So I gather you work. I'm interested in what you do."

Her brow lifted. "You mean, you don't already know?"

"No."

She sent him a wry look at the one-word answer. "My friend Angie owns a boutique and I work there three days a week."

"Have you been there long?"

"Long enough," she quipped, giving him a taste of his own medicine.

Just then, a curtain rolled back at the end of the dance floor to reveal a woman sitting at a piano. At the sound of applause, she burst into a song. Danielle appreciated the interruption and sent Flynn a wry smile, receiving a knowing look in return.

The songs continued while they ate their way through their meal, talking only sporadically. The singer had a very good voice so it was pleasant listening to her. Besides, it gave Danielle the chance to gather her thoughts before the next onslaught from Flynn.

Then the singing finished to further applause, but the woman continued to play. One of the couples rose from their table and strolled out to dance on the parquet floor, slipping into each other's arms as if they knew exactly where they were supposed to be in this world.

Then another couple followed and another. She didn't want Flynn to think *she* wanted to dance, so she looked down at her plate and began pushing the remaining salmon around with her fork.

"You're not hungry?

She glanced up and gave a polite smile. "It's delicious but I don't seem to have much of an appetite lately."

He placed his napkin beside his empty plate. "You'll have dessert."

She bristled slightly at the order. "None for me."

"But you've got to have something for your birthday. What about some of that chocolate concoction the woman over there is eating?"

Danielle glanced at the other table and felt sick at the thought of more chocolate. "No, I couldn't. Three o'clock this morning I was eating celery dipped in a jar of hazelnut chocolate. Lovely at the time but—"

"You should be doing other things at three in the morning," he suddenly growled, bringing sensuality back into focus. Without warning, he stood up. "Dance with me."

Her heart jumped in her throat as he helped her to her feet, then walked her out to the floor. She knew she

The Silhouette Reader Service™ — Here's how it works:

Accepting your 2 free books and 2 free mystery gifts places you under no obligation to buy anything. You may keep the books and gifts and return the shipping statement marked "cancel". If you do not cancel, about a month later we'll send you 6 additional books and bill you just $3.80 each in the U.S. or $4.47 each in Canada, plus 25¢ shipping & handling per book and applicable taxes if any.* That's the complete price and — compared to cover prices of $4.50 each in the U.S. and $5.25 each in Canada — it's quite a bargain! You may cancel at any time, but if you choose to continue, every month we'll send you 6 more books, which you may either purchase at the discount price or return to us and cancel your subscription.

*Terms and prices subject to change without notice. Sales tax applicable in N.Y. Canadian residents will be charged applicable provincial taxes and GST. All orders subject to approval. Credit or debit balances in a customer's account(s) may be offset by any other outstanding balance owed by or to the customer. Please allow 4 to 6 weeks for delivery.

GET FREE BOOKS and FREE GIFTS WHEN YOU PLAY THE...

SLOT MACHINE GAME!

Just scratch off the silver box with a coin. Then check below to see the gifts you get!

YES! I have scratched off the silver box. Please send me the 2 free Silhouette Desire® books and 2 free gifts for which I qualify. I understand I am under no obligation to purchase any books, as explained on the back of this card.

326 SDL ELYM   **225 SDL ELQA**

FIRST NAME	LAST NAME

ADDRESS

APT.#	CITY

STATE/PROV.	ZIP/POSTAL CODE

7	7	7	**Worth TWO FREE BOOKS plus 2 BONUS Mystery Gifts!**
🍒	🍒	🍒	**Worth TWO FREE BOOKS!**
♣	♣	♣	**Worth ONE FREE BOOK!**
🔔	🔔	🔔	**TRY AGAIN!**

www.eHarlequin.com

(S-D-05/07)

Offer limited to one per household and not valid to current Silhouette Desire® subscribers.

Your Privacy - Silhouette Books is committed to protecting your privacy. Our Privacy Policy is available online at www.eHarlequin.com or upon request from the Silhouette Reader Service. From time to time we make our lists of customers available to reputable firms who may have a product or service of interest to you. If you would prefer for us not to share your name and address, please check here ☐.

went into his arms as if she were made to be there, just like those other couples had with each other.

He pulled her close and she quivered and gave a small sigh, giving herself up to the moment, unable to fight him this one time. He smelled so good, so wonderful, so Flynn. His hand was against her back, caressing her, holding her against him, as if he'd never let her go.

Long moments crept by as they danced slowly around the dance floor, a possessive gleam in his eyes that both thrilled and disturbed her.

"Did you know your eyes turn smoky-blue at certain times?" he murmured thickly.

Her throat went dry. "When I'm angry?"

"When something moves you. When you get passionate."

Her breath caught in her lungs. "You shouldn't talk like that."

A muscle pulsated in his cheek. "We're adults, Danielle. We're allowed to talk any way we want." His arms tightened around her. "And do anything we want to do."

Her heart rate accelerated as if someone had pressed a button inside her and forgot to stop. There was a whole other subliminal conversation going on beneath their words…had been going on from the moment they'd met.

"I…um…need some fresh air," she said, her heart thudding against her ribs.

His gaze rested on her heated face. "Let's go for a walk."

"Ye—" she swallowed "—yes."

She didn't look at him as she let him take control, while

he paid the bill and ushered her through the restaurant and across the road to Bicentennial Park. She needed to get outside, to inhale some night air fresh from the ocean.

"Is this better?" Flynn asked as he tucked her arm through his and they began to stroll along the pavement.

"Yes, thank you. It was so hot in there." She glanced away when he sent her another knowing look.

As they walked, she forced herself to concentrate on her surroundings. The world had grown a little quieter at this hour. Older couples passed by, others headed home for the night. Younger people were just beginning to gather for the bar scene. Out on the ocean, lights from a distant boat bobbed in the water. Just behind them, the city's low skyline silhouetted itself against a black velvet sky.

And none of it could make Danielle forget that this virile man was beside her, the touch of his arm beneath her own shooting ripples of delight through her every step of the way.

Suddenly she noticed a commotion a few yards ahead and she automatically stopped dead. An old man was sitting on the pavement, crying. A younger man was trying to get him to stand up.

"Come on, Dad. Let's go home," the younger man said. "My car's just over there."

The father gave a sob. "I don't wanna go home, boyo. I wanna stay here."

"Dad, listen. You've got to come home. Mum's had enough. She can't take much more."

Danielle's heart went out to the son. The man obviously had a drinking problem. She went to hurry over to them, wanting to help if she could.

Flynn put a hand on her arm, stopping her. "Leave them."

Her eyes widened and her heart dipped with disappointment in him. She'd never been one to ignore a cry for help and she wasn't going to start now. "But they may need my—"

His face tightened. "They don't."

"Flynn, don't be silly."

"The man's an alcoholic, Danielle," he said harshly. "There's nothing you can do for him."

"But—"

"Let's leave his son with some dignity," he said, his face hardening as a crowd began to gather around the other couple.

The younger man looked up and she saw the despair and shame in his eyes. Flynn was right. He didn't need an audience.

"You don't belong in that world, Danielle," he said, taking her arm and leading her back toward his Mercedes.

She went without a murmur, the closed look in his eyes touching her deep inside, making her heart clench with a compassion she wouldn't have said he deserved a week ago. Instinctively, she knew he had done this before himself, probably as a boy with his own father. It explained a lot about Flynn. He must have been so hurt and humiliated all those years ago. No child should have to grow up like that.

They rode back to her apartment in silence, not even talking as they came out of the elevator and walked along the hallway. Danielle surprised herself by wanting to slip her arms around his waist and hold him tight, ease his heartache, but she knew it wouldn't be appreciated. He was a man who stood alone, no matter what the circumstances.

Their steps slowed as they reached her door. She swallowed as she turned to face him. "Flynn, about that man back there..."

"Forget him. I have."

No, this was important. "I want you to know...that I understand."

"Good." But he was suddenly looking at her lips.

She moistened them, not deliberately, but it didn't matter. She saw his eyes darken. "Thank you for dinner. It was a lovely evening."

He moved closer. "Nowhere near as lovely as you."

The breath hitched in her throat. She knew what he wanted. Knew the whole evening had been inching toward this in a silent, sensual way that had been sneaking up on both of them. "Flynn, no."

"No?" he said huskily.

She tilted her chin, trying to fight his attraction, trying *not* to reach out and touch him. "I can't let you make love to me."

He stilled. "Because of your pregnancy?"

"No. It's just that—"

He lifted his hand, ran a finger along her lower lip. "I want you more than I've ever wanted a woman, Danielle. Being with you tonight, having you in my arms, is driving me crazy."

She gasped as his finger left her mouth and slid down

the column of her throat. "There's some things…you can't have," she murmured, loving the feel of his touch against her skin. "I'm one of them."

He picked up the gold chain at her neck that had been her mother's and held it loosely between his fingers. "Tell me you don't want me," he challenged. "Give me a reason to walk away from you right now."

Her legs began to tremble as her stomach curled with need. "I…can't."

He dropped the chain against her skin, his finger sliding back up her neck, along her jawline. "I want you in my arms tonight, Danielle. I want the scent of you on me. But I want no regrets." His finger stilled under her chin, waiting.

She shuddered but she knew what she would do. She couldn't refuse him, not when every pore in her body was calling out to be embraced by him. Dear God, the only thing she'd regret right now was *not* making love to him.

"No regrets, Flynn," she whispered, and his eyes flared with white-hot heat. "Not tonight."

Tomorrow could take care of itself.

Six

Danielle's knees shook as she stepped inside her bedroom, with Flynn right behind her. She had no doubt this was meant to be, no doubt at all this was where she *wanted* to be, yet she was afraid.

Of herself.

Of Flynn.

Of the sheer breadth of sexual attraction between them.

"Look at me," he murmured and put his hand on her arm, slowly turning her around to face him, making sure she could see the very masculine look in his eyes that said he was all male, all possessive. That he wanted her. That he would have her. She could not deny him. Or herself.

"Flynn, I think…" She paused, suddenly not sure what she wanted to say.

"Don't think. Just feel, Danielle. *Feel* me touch you." His fingers began to stroke her arm through the thin material, the light touch so powerful it made her *feel* him, all right. She felt boneless as those dark, smoldering eyes held her in place while his hand slid up and cupped the curve of her shoulder, savored it before sliding his palm around to the back of her neck.

"Now come to me." He gently pulled her to him.

She went willingly, more than ready for his kiss, yet unprepared for the sensual onslaught he made on her mouth. For long moments his tongue brushed hers like a paintbrush to canvas, each touch adding more layers of sensation, intensifying with each caress, bringing her to life. She moaned at the taste of him, a combination of fine whiskey and a flavor that could only be Flynn.

He broke off the kiss and leaned back. "You are so beautiful," he said huskily, his eyes appraising her features, making her skin quiver, making her heart race, making her wonder how she'd existed before she knew of his touch.

His gaze traveled down to the creamy swell of her breasts. "I want to see all of you," he murmured, pushing her thin silky jacket from her shoulders, stripping away the layers of consciousness between them as the material slithered to the floor. Her dress followed and her stockings, leaving her in a black lacy bra and panties.

Suddenly she felt a little self-conscious. "This is embarrassing," she managed to say, quickly putting her hands across the front of herself, knowing it was useless to try and cover herself, but doing it all the same.

He moved her hands aside. "There's no need to hide from me, Danielle." Then he stilled, his piercing eyes riveting on her face. "Now it's just you and me. No one else."

She knew what he was saying. That the rest of the world, including her baby, had to take a backseat for the moment.

"I understand," she murmured.

Tiny flames leaped in his eyes and he began to make love to her in earnest. He undid her bra, letting it drop on top of the other clothes, then enlaced her breasts with warm hands that made her throat close off. His head lowered and his mouth suckled first one nipple then the next, drawing a moan from deep within her, making her burn with need. She curled her fingers through his hair and held him to her.

"It's not enough," she murmured, wanting to touch more of him. No, she *needed* to touch more of him. *All* of him. Her hands slid beneath his jacket, her palms smoothing over the hot skin under the material of his white shirt, spreading even more heat from his body to hers.

But before she could touch him further, he groaned and stepped back to pull his jacket off, rapidly followed by his shirt. Then he reached for the zipper of his trousers. She gave a small gasp as he stripped down to nothing before her very eyes.

Yet "nothing" could be further from the truth. He was magnificent, with a dark smattering of hair arrowing down his chest, over the rigid muscles of his stomach, to the irrefutable proof that he wanted her.

Heart beating wildly, she hesitated for a split second.

"You're gorgeous," she said, reaching for him, her hand sliding around his tight, hard erection to hold him as a lover. She watched with satisfaction as his jaw clenched and unclenched while she got to know him, heard the harsh uneven sound of his breathing when her thumb traced the smooth head of his arousal.

A shudder rumbled through him. "Enough! I want to pleasure *you*," he growled, taking her hands away and placing them on his chest, pulling her into his rip-cord arms. His eyes darkened with something primitive as he nudged her intimately, her thin panties the last barrier between them.

His mouth covered hers hungrily, and she kissed him in return until she felt the room twirl around her, until she could feel herself being guided, until the bed touched the back of her knees and she was suddenly helped down onto the mattress.

And then his lips began to trek a downward journey to where she melted for him. He whispered words of passion as he slid her panties down her legs, then kissed his way up them, teasing nerve endings along the inside of her calves, up along her inner thighs, before settling in to kiss her intimately. She gasped in sweet delight as Flynn marked her with his mouth.

Then his tongue stroked her, and her stirring pulse jumped to attention and rushed through her veins. He quickened his pace, and so did her pulse. She'd never felt more alive.

She wanted more.

More of this.

More of him.

More of everything.

But before she could burst with pleasure, he came up over her and nestled full length between her thighs, his arms supporting himself so he wouldn't lean on her too heavily.

He looked down at her, his eyes glittering with desire. "Are you sure?" he rasped, waiting, watching.

Her heart turned over as she looked up at the forceful planes of his face, knowing he wasn't the type of man to hesitate taking what he wanted, yet he hesitated with her.

"Come into me, Flynn," she said, her voice catching with the intensity of the moment.

He gave a low groan and parted her legs farther with his thighs. He entered her slowly, carefully, his eyes locked on hers. Those eyes devoured her as he set a slow sensuous rhythm, moving inside her with leisurely thrusts that were far from casual and built the tension inside her.

As if he felt it, too, he suddenly lowered his head and took her mouth by storm, and she gave her lips up to him as she had offered her body. He took it all, kissing her erotically, his tongue dipping in and out, around her lips, making a flush spread throughout her as his thrusts increased momentum, each movement sucking her more and more into a vortex of sensation.

And then sheer magic took over as she was sucked down and down, drowning in a shock wave of the most exquisite pleasure. She'd never felt this way before. Never suspected.

Then all thought left her as she fell into the deepest climax she'd ever had, every fiber in her body quivering around this man, quivering for him, *with* him.

Dear God, she never wanted it to end.

For a few seconds more, Flynn remained inside Danielle, leaning on his arms, looking down at the radiant picture she made beneath him. She was so soft to touch, so beautiful to look at, he didn't want to move away.

And he certainly didn't want other men knowing her like this, came an unbidden thought, as an intense streak of possessiveness filled him. She was *his,* for as long as he wanted her, and right now that was going to be quite a while. A man couldn't make love to a woman like Danielle and not want to keep her as his own.

Except she was pregnant.

Pregnant with another man's child.

And she hadn't hesitated to use that to her advantage.

Just then she moved slightly and he pushed his thoughts aside, determined to ignore them. There were other things to think about when he had a sexy woman in his arms. "Are you okay?"

"Wonderful," she murmured, her eyes sensuously drowsy.

He was tempted to arouse her again, but he could see she was tired and needed a rest. Giving her a hard kiss, he rolled onto his back, pulling her close to his side, her head resting in the curve of his arm. She fit snugly against him.

"Flynn, I'm so…" her eyelids fluttered shut "…tired."

"Sleep," he said, and kissed the top of her head, then heard her breathing soften and deepen as she fell into a deep slumber.

He lay there for a long time, thinking about this woman in his arms and what it meant that she had given herself to him. If he hadn't known she was a con artist, he would have said she wasn't a woman who would give herself lightly. He would have said she'd have to care about him in some small way to be lying here like this with him. And he definitely would have said that for her it wouldn't just be about sexual attraction.

Not the way it was for him.

He swallowed hard and knew he was lying to himself. He found Danielle deeply attractive, but he had also begun to care about her in spite of himself. Yet it was a feeling he didn't appreciate or want, and with the same determination that had taken him from a pauper to a very rich man, he put his emotions aside to concentrate on what was important. And that was right here, right now.

During the night he reached for her and they made love again, and this time *he* was the one who fell heavily asleep as soon as it was over.

But he still knew when she slipped out of bed in the early hours of the morning. In the moonlight he watched her pad naked to the bathroom across the hall, his body stirring even before she'd closed the door behind her.

He waited for her return, the bed feeling big and empty.

Right at that moment the bathroom door opened and he caught a glimpse of her dressed in her bathrobe before she flicked the light off. Good heavens. Did she think a bit of material would stop him from wanting her? Stop him needing her in his arms?

But instead of coming back to bed, she quietly went and opened a drawer and took out some clothes. He knew then what she was up to. His mouth thinned. She was about to sneak out without waking him and go into another room to spend the rest of the night. Perhaps on the sofa.

And the next time he saw her she would have put up that wall of reserve again. He wouldn't allow it.

"Come back to bed, Danielle."

Startled, her gaze flew across to him. "Flynn! I thought you were asleep."

He leaned up on his elbow, letting her know he was wide-awake and not about to let her run away. "You thought wrong."

"I was just going to—"

"Take that robe off and come back to bed," he murmured, lifting the sheet, aching to make love to her, but prepared to let her sleep if need be.

She hesitated.

"Danielle," he said firmly, not prepared to wait any longer.

She placed her bundle of clothes on the dresser and quickly undid the robe, dropping it from her shoulders, exposing her glorious naked body to him, making him catch his breath.

Then she slid in next to him and he pulled her up close. His heart thumped when she curled her fingers through his chest hair in silent invitation, and soon she had him making love to her, until she begged him to take her again and he could no more deny her than deny himself. Afterward, they fell into a deep sleep in each other's arms.

He awoke to find her still in his arms, the side of her face pressed against his chest. He decided he liked waking up next to a beautiful woman like Danielle. In fact, he rather liked the idea of having her in his bed all the time.

She began to stir. The sheet covered her shoulders but didn't quite hide her bare breasts, a sight he enjoyed as she stretched, her leg sliding along his own, thigh rubbing against thigh, her fingers flexing out over his stomach, fanning lower.

She froze and her eyes flew open. For a moment he saw the confusion, then a flush began to rise up her throat and into her cheeks. Her reaction was just a simple thing, but it told him she was no longer used to being in a man's arms like this. The thought warmed him.

And then she pushed against him and tried to sit up. "Um…I think you'd better leave."

He scowled and held her still, making her look at him. "We said no regrets, Danielle."

She shook her head. "It's not that. It's Monica. If she comes by… If she sees you here…like this…" She winced.

All at once he realized Danielle was frightened of her mother-in-law. She may not admit it to herself, but it was there.

And after the little episode he'd had with Monica himself yesterday morning, he shouldn't have been surprised. The older woman definitely had a way of disturbing people.

Hell, the woman was *disturbed,* herself. And if she thought Danielle had gotten involved with him—worse, was sleeping with him—she'd be more than disturbed. Seeing Danielle's reaction now, it suddenly didn't seem so far-fetched for Monica to hurt her and the baby. And he knew he could only protect them so much. He swallowed hard. God, if Monica hurt either one of them, he'd never forgive himself.

A though crystallized inside him.

"Marry me."

Her head had gone back, her eyes wide in astonishment. "Wh-what!"

"I want you to marry me." All at once he felt he was doing the right thing.

She pushed herself away from him. "I don't believe I'm hearing this," she whispered, disbelief ringing the irises of her blue eyes.

"Why not?" When she had time to think about it, he was sure she'd come around to the proposal.

"First you accuse me of trying to get you to marry me for the sake of my baby, now you *want* me to marry you?"

"Prerogative is not only the domain of the female." The more he thought about it, the more the idea was growing on him. Surprisingly, he didn't care that she wasn't quite the woman he wanted her to be. Being a gold digger was one hell of a fault in her, but he would cope with that. He'd make sure he kept her under control. But he had to protect her from Monica.

"But you think I'm a liar and cheat. You've accused me of trying to get all I can out of you." Her eyes held a sudden wary look. "What's changed your mind?"

He didn't miss a beat. "Nothing a prenuptial agreement couldn't solve." If she suspected it was because of Monica, she would refuse his offer. "Oh, and I'd want it in writing that you'll remain faithful to me, of course."

"Gee, thanks."

He ignored that. He had the money to keep her in the lifestyle she obviously enjoyed. And if he made her sign the prenuptial and watched her like a hawk so that she couldn't get herself into trouble, then they could have a good life together.

The alternative was suddenly unthinkable.

She shook her head. "This is about honor, isn't it? You feel you have to do the honorable thing."

He had to smile. "I've made love to many women but I didn't feel I had to marry any of them."

Her eyes narrowed with suspicion. "Then it's because I'm pregnant."

"I'd ask you to marry me whether you were pregnant or not." That was the truth. Pregnant or not, he needed to protect her at all costs.

Always.

She sat up against the pillows, pulling the sheet up under her chin, her eyes confused. "I don't understand."

He started to speak but then thought better of it. He may have feelings for this woman but he wasn't yet ready to lay them on the line. He'd always played his cards close to his chest and he would do the same here.

"Simple. It's time I got married."

"And the woman you consider a fortune hunter is the chosen one? How nice."

He ignored her sarcasm as he swung his legs over the side of the bed. "I'm getting older. And you're the first woman I can imagine waking up with for the next twenty years."

"So it's not a lifetime guarantee?" she quipped.

He acknowledged her wit with a thin smile as he looked back at her. "I was speaking figuratively."

She shot him a speculative glance. "You would want children?" she said, as if testing him.

His smile vanished into thin air as the memory of his mother dying in childbirth all those years ago came to mind. His jaw clenched and his heart slammed against his ribs. He'd sworn never to have children. Sworn never to risk a woman's life for the sake of procreation.

But now that pledge had been taken out of his hands. Danielle was going to have her baby whether he feared for her life or not. So he would make sure she got the best medical care. These days it would be highly unlikely for a woman to die in childbirth, he reassured himself.

"Of course I want more children," he said brusquely. "With you."

Her hand went to her stomach, as if in protection. "And what about *this* baby?"

That previous sense of protectiveness rose up inside him. "I would bring the child up as my own."

Her bare shoulders tensed. "But would you love my baby as your own?"

"Yes." And he would. Every child should be valued

and protected and, this child, being Danielle's child, would be more than special.

Her shoulders relaxed a little, but she continued to stare at him as if she couldn't quite believe this was happening.

Then a look of panic crossed her face and she threw back the covers, attempting to push herself off the bed. "No. I'm sorry. I can't marry you. I don't want to marry anyone."

Her previous marriage must have still reminded her of unpleasant things. And that reminded him of Monica. His stomach clenched tightly as he stood up and strode around the bed to help her.

He tried a change in tactic. "Think of it this way. If you married me, you would never have to worry about money again. I can give you everything you need."

She flinched, then ignoring his outstretched hand, she pushed to her feet and went to pick up her robe from the floor. Saving her the trouble, he scooped the robe up and held it open for her, taking pleasure in her naked figure as she quickly slid into it.

"Once I sign an agreement, right?" She didn't wait for him to answer. "You're as calculating as my husband."

Displeasure furrowed his brow. "Don't you mean your *late* husband?"

She began to speak then stopped.

For some reason, the culmination of her comments about Robert Ford hit him in the gut. "What did he do to you, Danielle?"

Her eyes flashed with remembered pain. Then she said, "Nothing."

"Tell me. I'd like to know."

She held his gaze for a moment, then as if believing his sincerity, she took a shaky breath. "He smothered me, Flynn. Smothered me until I couldn't make a move without him. Until I couldn't breathe. He was very much like his mother in that respect."

His jaw knotted, not liking the picture she painted. Now more than ever he was glad he'd proposed marriage. He had to get Danielle away from her mother-in-law. "Perhaps he wanted to spoil you?" he suggested, not for a moment believing that was true. Not after having met Robert Ford.

"Spoil me?" she scoffed. "By making sure I never got a moment to myself? By criticizing everything I did? By sucking the life out of me?" She shook her halo of blond hair. "No, the only one who was spoiled was Robert, only I didn't see that when I first married him."

Flynn began to burn for her. "*I* wouldn't do that to you."

She shuddered, the look in her eyes clutching at his heart. "You're doing it already. Flynn, I only went to bed with you. I didn't expect a proposal of marriage."

He forced himself to relax. He would show her that things would be different with him. He would prove it to her, if she let him. "I'm not asking you to cut off an arm, Danielle."

Her lips twisted. "At least that would be quicker than the slow torture of being smothered to death."

Dammit, her husband had made the mistakes, not *him*. He wasn't about to pay for the faults of another man, especially a dead one.

"You won't get a better offer," he pointed out.

She shot him a cold look. "I don't *want* a better offer. I don't want any offer at all." She headed for the bathroom door, then stopped and glanced over her shoulder. "And, Flynn, this isn't the beginning of an affair. This is the end of it."

He watched her go, heard the click of the lock behind her, but not for a minute did he agree that this was the end for them. He hadn't got where he was by giving up on something he wanted badly. And right now he not only wanted to protect Danielle and her baby, but all at once he wanted Danielle in his life, as crazy as it sounded.

And he always got what he wanted.

Seven

Danielle leaned her hands on the bathroom sink for support and swallowed away the lump in her throat. *Marriage!*

How could Flynn do this to her? How could he take something so beautiful like their lovemaking last night and spoil it with a proposal of marriage? He had to be the last person she'd expect to want to marry her. The last person who'd want to tie himself down. After all, he was a virile man who was sure to have a string of women more willing and able.

Yet he wanted *her*.

The supposed gold digger.

The supposed fortune hunter.

The supposed woman who would do anything to get his attention.

She just didn't understand it. But it didn't matter anyway. Dear God, she couldn't go through another marriage to a man who needed to possess her for the sake of possession. She wouldn't be able to breathe again. Just thinking about it made her throat tighten. All she wanted was her independence.

But she *had* to think about it, in case she found herself weakening toward Flynn. She had to remember and be strong. She must never forget what Robert had done to her in the name of love. Never forget Robert wanting to know where she was every minute of the day, even when she was at work. Never forget the "suggestions" of what to wear, not just by Robert but his mother. Nor the criticism whenever she'd given an opinion, until she'd given no opinion at all.

She'd been young when she'd married, too young, really. And she'd been looking to fall in love when she'd met Robert. She'd missed her parents and had wanted someone to love her back.

But she'd chosen the wrong man, the wrong family, and by the time she'd discovered that, it had been too late. She'd married Robert Ford.

And his mother.

And Flynn wanted her to walk back into the fire? There was no way she would make that mistake again. No amount of sex, no matter how fantastic, would be enough to get her to marry him.

Thankfully Flynn had gone by the time she came out of the bathroom, and Danielle escaped for a stroll through the botanical gardens, appreciating the cooler lushness of the tropical surrounds in the steady heat of the day. But it did nothing to ease her mind, though she kept looking over her shoulder as she walked. She had the feeling someone was watching her, but she soon dismissed the thought. If Flynn were anywhere near her, she'd know about it. And then she spent the rest of Sunday at home on edge that Flynn would come back and put pressure on her to accept his proposal of marriage.

What nerve he had.

Not that she doubted for a moment she would give in, but she wasn't really prepared to withstand him right now, not after their night of lovemaking. And she wouldn't put it past him to use their sexual attraction to try and get a promise of marriage out of her, either.

She'd fought too hard to get to this point in her life, pregnant or not, and the last thing she wanted was to trap a man into marriage. *She* would be the one who'd be trapped…trapped by a man who obviously thought of women as useful for one thing only.

Thank heavens she *was* pregnant. The very thing that Mr. Flynn Donovan feared was the one thing that would save her from his clutches.

Her baby.

In the end he never came by, neither did Monica, and she had an uneventful day preparing her clothes for work and cleaning the apartment. Afterward she rearranged the furniture in the baby's room, then sorted through the pile of baby clothes Angie's friend had given her.

Her hands trembled as she lifted the little vests and jumpsuits. So tiny and sweet. She found it hard to imagine something so small would even fit into them. Even harder to believe she was carrying that baby inside her and in six months she would be holding her child in her arms. She'd tried to prepare but there was no doubt a baby would make a huge difference in her life.

Unfortunately she *wasn't* prepared for a bombshell the next day at work. Ben Richmond, the Realtor who'd offered her the apartment, called her at the boutique midmorning while Angie was out doing some bank business.

"Danielle, do you think I could come and see you? It's important."

"What is it, Ben?" Something was wrong. She could tell by his tone.

"How about I come by in an hour? Does that suit you?"

"Yes," she agreed, but once she hung up the telephone she worried about what the problem could be. Ben had been so guarded on the phone.

He was even less cheerful when he pushed open the door to the store and saw her standing beside a row of clothes. His gaze behind the horn-rimmed glasses immediately dropped to her stomach, then back up to her face. "I'm sorry to ask you this, Danielle, but are you pregnant?"

Danielle frowned. "Yes, but—"

He winced then shook his graying head. "So you're having a baby?" he said, as if he still didn't want to believe it.

Frowning, she glanced down at her black trousers and sleeveless, body-hugging, cream-colored top that gave no hint of the baby beneath her stomach. "What's that got to do with anything?"

A momentary look of discomfort crossed his face. "I

hate to tell you this, but the lease you signed said no children." He held out his hands in a helpless gesture and shrugged. "I'm sorry, but there it is."

"Wh-what?" Her legs threatened to buckle and she made her way to one of the chairs.

Ben shot her a sympathetic glance. "If it were up to me, I'd let you stay. Unfortunately your landlord called us this morning after receiving a complaint from one of the other tenants and that leaves us no choice."

Danielle tried to take it all in. "Are you telling me I have to *leave* my apartment? My home?"

He gave an encouraging smile. "Don't worry. We're not going to kick you out tomorrow or anything." His smile faded. "But the landlord *is* insisting that you leave as soon as possible. He sincerely apologizes but he has no choice, either."

"But…but…I don't remember that clause in my lease." She'd been so grateful to be moving in she hadn't read it thoroughly.

"It's there, but I can't let you take all the blame. I should have pointed it out. I just didn't think about it because I knew you and Rob didn't have any children. I didn't realize you were already pregnant."

Her fingers fluttered to her neck. "It took so long to find something suitable that I jumped at it without thinking." Tears pricked her eyes. "Now I've got to find somewhere else to live."

Ben looked worried. "Don't upset yourself. I'll help you. I've got a couple of places in mind not far from where you are now. You'll like them, I promise."

The thought of moving again filled her with dread.

What if they couldn't find somewhere suitable? She'd have to return to Monica's.

"Are you all right?"

His words stopped her panic in its tracks. She took a deep breath and straightened her shoulders. One step at a time. She'd manage.

"I'll be okay."

Ben's face relaxed with relief. "Why don't I call you tomorrow? We'll go take a look at some other apartments."

She tried to smile. It wasn't his fault she'd been so careless. "Fine."

His eyes filled with regret. "I'm so sorry about this, Danielle."

"I know." She started to rise.

"No, you stay there. I'll see myself out." He walked to the door.

All at once, she just had to know. "Ben, I don't suppose you can tell me who complained?"

He stopped and turned. "I honestly don't know. The landlord called my boss about it. That's all he would tell me." Ben left just as a woman customer entered the shop. The woman looked at her oddly, but Danielle couldn't risk a smile so she stood up and went back behind the counter, leaving the woman to browse.

But as the numbness wore off she tried to think who was the culprit. The yuppie couple on the first floor? The businesswoman living next door to them?

Danielle automatically knew all of them would hate the thought of a baby living in the building, crying at all hours of the night. Why, even Flynn would object to…

She sucked in a sharp breath. Was it Flynn who had called her landlord? Would he stoop so low? She swallowed as something horrifying occurred to her. Had his intention been to force her into marrying him?

Suddenly it all made sense and she felt sick to her stomach. How could he do this to her? They'd shared a night together and now he thought he could manipulate her. She wouldn't put any dirty tricks past him. God, were all men swines?

Just then, Angie returned. Not wanting to worry her friend who had enough on her plate, somehow Danielle managed to act normal as she stood up and said she needed to go out for a short while. Angie gave her a searching glance, mentioned that Danielle looked pale and asked if she was okay, then said to take the rest of the day off if she wanted. Danielle politely refused, though she was grateful for the offer.

And then she left the store and walked to an office block in the city center. Flynn Donovan was in for a surprise today. And she could guarantee he wouldn't like it.

Only, when she reached his office, his secretary apologized and said he'd gone home to change before flying out to Paris later this afternoon.

Danielle swallowed hard, feeling the tears threaten. She was about to lose her home and the instigator was leaving town.

The older woman frowned. "Look, let me give you his address. I'm sure he'll be happy to see you."

Danielle knew that was one thing he *wouldn't* be, but she couldn't say that, in case the woman withdrew the offer. She just hoped the secretary didn't get into trouble on her behalf.

"That's very kind of you."

"I'm glad to help." The woman smiled encouragingly. "You'd better hurry. I'd hate for you to miss him."

So would she.

Ten minutes later she stopped her car in front of one of the houses along the waterfront, thankful she could see Flynn's Mercedes parked on the paved driveway. She glanced up at the luxurious, two-story residence with its expansive glass windows absorbing the view of the sea. Anyone who owned this placed never had to worry about having somewhere to live.

Not like her, she thought, pushing aside her despair as she got out of her car and stormed up to the house. She was just reaching the dozen or so steps when the front door swung open and there stood Flynn with an older couple behind him. For a moment she was disconcerted.

Then she remembered why she was here.

"There you are, you coward!"

To say Flynn was surprised by the woman on his doorstep was an understatement, but he didn't show it. What on earth was Danielle doing here? She hadn't just dropped by for a friendly visit, not with those lovely blue eyes blazing at him beneath pencil-slim brows, her glossy lips thin with anger, her chin tilted at an irate angle. She looked beautiful and feisty.

"Danielle," he growled, stepping through the doorway toward her as she reached the top step. "Perhaps you should come inside."

"Oh, that's right. Be polite. Let's not disillusion your

staff about the type of boss they have." Her furious gaze swept over the older couple. "I bet you think he's a decent human being. Well, so did I and look where it got me?" She slammed her hands on slim hips covered by a clingy top. "I'm pregnant and Flynn Donovan doesn't care if I have this baby out on the street."

He swore under his breath. "I don't know what your problem is but I suggest we talk about this in private." Taking her by the elbow, he marched her inside past Louise and Thomas, then closed his study door behind them and turned to face her.

His eyes narrowed. "Now. What the hell is wrong with you? And what's all this about you having the baby out on the street?"

She shot him a hostile glare. "Don't pretend you don't know."

His mouth set in a tight line. "I'm not pretending. I haven't the faintest idea what you're going on about."

"You told my landlord about me having a baby, didn't you? You must have found out children aren't allowed to live in the building." Her voice suddenly broke on an emotional note. "Now I—" she swallowed, her eyes glistening "—now I have to leave."

"You think I'd do that?" he rasped, striding toward her but she quickly stepped back, refusing to let him come any closer. He stopped a few feet away.

Her chin set in a stubborn line as she blinked back the tears. "Absolutely."

"Even after last night?" he said in a brusque tone, a growing heaviness centering in his chest.

"*Especially* after last night," she said without hesitation.

He drew himself up straighter, taut with anger. "I'm sorry but I don't see the connection."

"Then you're the only one. You made me homeless so I'd have to marry you."

He flinched inwardly. Was this the same woman he'd made love to last night? The same woman who had slid back into bed with him and begged him to make love to her?

"Danielle, you have my word that I had nothing to do with this."

But he knew who did.

Monica.

Thank heavens he'd put a guard on her yesterday as soon as he'd left her apartment…a woman who knew she'd better do a good job or else…until he could get back from Paris and protect Danielle himself.

Her eyes distrusted him but he saw a flicker of doubt. "How can I believe that?"

He drew himself up straighter. "In business, my word would be enough."

"This isn't business. This is personal." As soon as she said the words, she flushed, a becoming tint highlighting her cheekbones.

"Yes, very personal," he drawled, pleased by her reaction.

"You know I don't mean it like that," she said, her voice softer now, the look in her eyes more gentle.

His gut clenched. "I can't help what you think about me, but getting someone thrown out on the street is not my style."

She stared, her eyes assessing him as the seconds

ticked by. Then her mouth relaxed a fraction. "Why do I believe you?"

Fierce relief launched through his veins. "Because you know it's the truth," he said, pulling her toward him, the scent of Allure perfume filling his nostrils, stirring his senses. He hardened with desire and pressed himself against her, letting her feel what she did to him.

Her eyes darkened and she shuddered, her body emitting an aura that curled around him. "No," she mumbled, pushing out of his arms and spinning toward the study window, where she stood with her back to him.

"You're fighting a losing battle, Danielle."

She let out a slow breath and turned to face him. "There isn't going to be any battle," she said, deliberately misreading him. "They're the ones calling the shots. I have to leave the apartment. I have no choice."

He was about to ignore her comment when something occurred to him, making him angry just thinking about it. "Surely the person who got you the apartment in the first place should have told you about the no-children policy," he snapped.

She shot him a withering glance. "For your information Ben is a friend of Robert's and, no, he didn't know about the baby. And by the way, he's a Realtor, not an ex-lover." She winced. "I think he felt sorry for me living with Monica."

Strangely enough, he suspected she was telling the truth. Yet could she really believe this Ben didn't have other intentions? He was a man and any male would have carnal thoughts of Danielle and bed.

He forced his hands to unclench. "Do you know who told the landlord you were pregnant?"

"No."

God. She really had no idea, no suspicion that Monica would do this to her. Danielle didn't deserve a mother-in-law who tried to get her thrown out on the street.

Actually it was probably because of *him* that Monica was being so vindictive in the first place. He'd stirred the older woman up and now she was taking it out on Danielle.

All at once he stilled as another angle to this occurred to him, just the way it did in his business dealings. Any attempt by Monica to get her daughter-in-law back was bound to send Danielle running in the other direction.

Toward *him*.

Hmm. This may end up better than he'd thought.

"What does it matter now, anyway?" Danielle said, but her eyes flickered with uncertainty. "The damage is done. Ben said he would find me something else."

He gritted his teeth. This Ben sounded far too helpful for his liking. "You could fight it."

"What's the use? Others in the building obviously don't want me there." Full-blown pride angled her chin. "And I'd rather not stay where I'm not wanted."

He hated to see her hurting this way and once again he realized there was more depth to this woman than he'd previously believed. "I know a place where you're wanted," he said pointedly. "Very much."

She held his gaze, lifted her chin more. "Thank you for your concern but I'll be fine."

His jaw tautened. "Come on. I'll take you home."

"I have my car."

"I won't have you driving while you're upset. My car's out front."

"Don't you have a plane to Paris to catch?"

Connie must have told her, including giving Danielle his address. Not that he minded.

He glanced at the gold Rolex on his wrist. He could delay the meeting or send someone else, preferably the latter. "I won't be going now."

"Oh, but—"

"I'm taking you home."

Despair crossed her face. "Flynn, I don't need you to drive me home. I can manage."

"No." He reached for the door handle, then looked at her. An odd tenderness swelled inside him. "Sit down and relax for a minute. I'll be back shortly."

As soon as Danielle stepped inside the penthouse and looked around what had so quickly become her home, a sense of despair filled her. Tears sprang to her eyes. She would miss this spacious apartment, with its glorious view of the ocean, sweeping around to the city skyline and backdropped by the brightest of blue skies.

Yet it wasn't about the luxury. This was her new beginning. She felt safe here. Safe and secure.

And now it had come to an end.

Flynn tugged her toward him, and for once she knew she needed to lean on someone. On him. It would be the last time, she promised herself as she went willingly into his arms. They were surprisingly comforting and full of a strength that seemed to pour into her and helped her blink back the tears.

"Sorry," she mumbled against his shirt, hating to cry even a little. It was just those silly hormones again.

"No need to apologize," he said, his deep voice rumbling in her ears.

She sniffed and leaned back to look up at him. Right at that moment she realized it wasn't just this apartment that made her feel safe and secure. It was being in Flynn's arms, too. She felt protected, as she'd never been protected before. But in a good way, unlike with Robert.

Robert. A sensation tightened her throat as she pushed away bad memories and concentrated on now. She was about to lose her home.

"Oh, Flynn, I thought this place would be mine for a few years at least. It's going to be so hard to leave."

He reached out and tucked a strand of hair behind her ear. "Try not to worry about it."

She frowned. "How can I *not* worry? I signed a lease in good faith. I never, ever sign anything without reading it first. I wouldn't even sign that paperwork Robert insisted..." All at once she remembered.

He stilled, but his eyes had grown alert. "Are you talking about the paperwork for the loan?"

Her breath stopped. Dear God, if she told him the truth would he tell Monica? Could she beg him not to? Could she throw herself on his mercy for the sake of her child? Of course she could.

"Danielle?" he warned in a low voice that said this was very important.

She totally agreed.

"Yes, Flynn, I *am* talking about that loan," she admitted, stepping back, needing to separate herself from him while she talked. "I knew nothing about it. In fact, looking back I can see that Robert tried to get me to sign the paperwork but I felt uncomfortable so I threw it away. I never heard another thing until you sent me that letter and even then I didn't realize Robert had forged my signature. Not until I saw it on the contract you showed me." She took a ragged breath. "But why believe me now when you didn't believe me before?"

A muscle pulsated in his lean cheek. "I know you now and I believe you're telling me the truth."

She choked back a short laugh. "How magnanimous of you."

"I deserve that, but why didn't you insist on telling me the truth before?" His gaze narrowed on her. "What are you trying to hide, Danielle?"

She sent him a wary glance. "I thought you might go to Monica and ask her for the money," she admitted uneasily, praying she was doing the right thing. "That's why I kept sending you those checks. I couldn't risk her knowing. You see, if you didn't believe me about the forged signature then she might prefer not to, as well. I knew she would use any opportunity to take this baby away from me." She hugged her stomach protectively. "She still could. She'd drag me through the courts until my name was mud and she had my child in her custody."

"Over my dead body," he snarled.

Her throat seemed to close up but she managed to say, "Thank you."

"This is why you were agitated when Monica came

to your door, isn't it? You thought I might mention the money to her."

She nodded. "I was trying to get you out of there as fast as I could."

"Danielle, I wouldn't have mentioned the money then and you have no need to fear I will tell her now. That woman would be the last person in the world I'd want to raise a child. Any child. And definitely not *your* child."

She swallowed a lump in her throat, blinked back sudden tears, then straightened her shoulders. "Unfortunately none of this fixes my immediate problem."

He considered her. "Why not just wait and see what happens?"

That was easy to say when a person had plenty of money the way he did. He could afford to move into a hotel. She grimaced. He could afford to *buy* the hotel.

"No, I have to face reality now. It's no use burying my head in the sand."

"We'll figure something out. Trust me."

We? He planned on helping her? *Again.* That was why he wasn't too worried on her behalf.

She took a shuddering breath and faced him. "Flynn, in case I haven't made it clear, I do *not* need your help."

"If you married me at least you wouldn't have to worry about having nowhere to live."

She gasped, dismayed he was back on that subject again. "I *will* have somewhere to live. Ben said—"

"Forget Ben! He's going to stick you in a tiny apartment in some run-down part of Darwin somewhere."

She boldly met his gaze. "It doesn't appear to have done *you* any harm."

Anger flared then died in his eyes. "Not quite everyone from my street turned themselves into a millionaire," he drawled.

"Oh, you mean, no one but you and your friends have the brains to do what you've done?" she said sarcastically.

"Marry me."

She tensed. "No."

"You'll be very happy. I promise."

"Don't make a promise you might not keep."

A muscle knotted in his jaw. "Do you want your child to suffer without a father?" he asked harshly.

She gasped. "That's not fair. I plan on being the best parent a child can have."

"But you had parents. Plural. Are you going to deny your child something he should automatically have?"

Her chin lifted. "Maybe I'll marry one day, but to the right man. That's not you."

He swore low in his throat.

"This is harassment, Flynn."

"Wanting someone is *not* harassment."

"You used sex to get what you can't have. *Me*." She shot him a shrewd look. "And I find it oddly telling that you haven't mentioned anything about love."

He didn't move a muscle. "I'd prefer not to start off our marriage with high expectations."

"I…am…*not*…marrying…you," she said with gritted teeth.

"I'm sure we'll learn to love each other in our own way over time," he said, ignoring her protest. "For now, our desires will give us a few years grace. We'll make a good marriage together."

"No, we won't."

His mouth thinned with displeasure. "Danielle, I'm not arguing." He went to reach for her but she spun away.

Only, she spun too fast and without warning she felt dizzy. Too dizzy. Her knees felt weak and nausea was rising up her throat. She could hear the blood pounding in her ears.

"Flynn," she whispered, and suddenly he was there, his arms around her, holding her, his presence comforting.

"Danielle?"

She rested her head on his shoulder and heard him say her name in a worried tone, but she was too busy trying to stop the world from spinning.

His arms tightened a little. "I'm here, sweetheart."

A moment passed, then another and thankfully the dizziness started to ease, the nausea abating, the blood not pounding quite as loudly in her ears.

"Are you okay?" he murmured, his heart thudding against her cheek.

She pushed back a little and looked up at him. "Yes," she said on a shaky breath. "I felt a little faint, that's all."

"This is happening far too often." He swooped her up in his arms and headed for her bedroom. "I'm calling my doctor. And I don't want any argument from you."

This time Danielle didn't *want* to argue. For all her talk about independence, she knew he was right. She hadn't been feeling right lately, so another checkup by a doctor was in order. She didn't want to risk losing the baby. She couldn't. Her baby was the only thing worthwhile in her life. She would be heartbroken if anything happened.

"How do you feel now?" Flynn said after he'd made her comfortable on the bed, then called the doctor on his cell phone.

The concern in his eyes halted her inner panic. "Better."

He sat down next to her on the bed and squeezed her hand, as if trying to instill strength into her. "I won't let anything happen to you or the baby," he assured her.

She looked at his grim mouth and pale face and her heart softened. "Flynn, you can't stop it."

"Don't," he muttered, and she realized he was taking this much too personally. But she knew all about regrets and she wasn't about to let either of them take responsibility for this.

Her throat thickened. "You can't blame yourself for my feeling faint."

"I shouldn't have tried to grab you like that."

"You weren't being rough, Flynn. You never are."

He held her gaze. "Thank you for that."

The softened look in his eyes made her heart tumble over and she almost wanted to faint again, but for a different reason. "Um…how long do you think the doctor will be?"

Arrogance returned to his face. "Bloody quick, if he knows what's good for him."

She had to smile, glad to see the old Flynn back. And for the first time she actually noticed his marine-blue polo shirt and gray chinos that made him look both casual and sophisticated. There was something very distracting about the way the fine material of his shirt hugged his shoulders. Far too distracting.

All at once he kissed her hard on the mouth then jumped to his feet. "I'll get you a drink of water. Call out if you need me."

She watched him walk away, tempted to call out and say that she *did* need him, but that might be admitting too much, even in jest. He'd use it to his advantage at some time or other, no doubt.

When the middle-aged doctor came, he was introduced as Mike. She reddened when Flynn stood by watching her being examined.

Mike straightened. "The baby's fine."

Sheer relief washed over her. "Thank God," she said, seeing the same reflection on Flynn's face.

The doctor eyed her. "Have you had any stress lately? Getting enough sleep? Eating right?"

"She's had a lot of stress, Mike," Flynn said, and she shot him a look that said she could speak for herself.

Mike frowned. "Hmm, then I hope you don't live here alone."

"Yes, she does," Flynn said again before she could get a word in. She glared at him again.

"Not a good idea." The doctor put his stethoscope away and clicked the bag shut. "Don't you have a friend or relative you could move in with for a while? You need to rest. Otherwise I might have to put you in the hospital," he said, making her gasp. "It would only be a precautionary measure," he assured her.

"She'll be staying at my place," Flynn said with authority, sending her heart slamming against her ribs.

"Excellent," Mike approved. "But you must take it easy from now on, young lady. You need to eat properly and rest. No work for a week and be careful after that." He glanced at Flynn. "You can continue intimate relations. That shouldn't be a problem."

Flynn inclined his head. "Good."

Sharp anxiety was twisting inside Danielle, so she didn't pay much attention to the rest of the conversation. Then something occurred to her.

She waited until the doctor left before sending Flynn an accusing stare. "You two planned this, didn't you?"

Surprise, then annoyance crossed Flynn's face. "Perhaps I should call Mike back? I'm sure he'd love to hear his integrity being questioned like this." He paused. "Not to mention my own."

She grimaced. "Okay, so I got it wrong."

"You're moving in with me. You're sick and not well enough to look after yourself. And you need to move out of this penthouse permanently."

She could feel herself being swallowed up again by him and his tactics. "I won't be your mistress, Flynn. I have my child to think about. No. I'll find another place."

His eyes flashed at her. "And then what? I leave you alone so you could possibly die?"

The breath caught in her throat. "Don't exaggerate. I'm fine. Mike just said so."

All at once, the anger seemed to leave him. His eyes clouded over. "Allow me to do this for you and the baby, Danielle."

She realized he still felt guilty. She swallowed the lump

in her throat. Seeing this side to him softened her, made her admit to herself that he was in an awkward position.

But she was torn whichever way she went. If she stayed at her apartment it would only be temporary. And she would still have to look for a new apartment as well as go to work. She'd probably make herself sicker, perhaps even risk having a miscarriage.

But if she went to Flynn's place, would he see it as a sign that she was weakening toward marriage? Perhaps they could come to a temporary truce.

"Okay, I'll move in, Flynn, but only until I have the baby." Then she'd go back to work full-time and get her own place, away from Monica and definitely away from Flynn.

Deep satisfaction showed in his eyes, but it was the barely perceptible easing of his shoulders that somehow reassured her in her decision.

"You're doing the right thing," he said.

"For who, Flynn? You or me?"

"For your baby."

Eight

When Danielle stepped inside Flynn's mansion, she was introduced to Louise and Thomas, the older couple she'd seen there earlier in the day. They'd known Flynn a long time and looked after him and his house, and Danielle had no doubt *she* was included in the package now.

But when she found that Flynn had hired a nurse to keep an eye on her, she almost turned around and walked out the door. It was too much. Everything was happening too fast. Suddenly the enormity of the day overwhelmed her and she felt tears sting her eyes.

The middle-aged nurse took in the situation quickly. "Come on, pet. Let's get you to bed."

Thankfully Flynn didn't follow them up the sweeping staircase and into a superbly furnished bedroom, and once she was in bed Danielle began to relax under Jean's professional but sympathetic eyes. She fell asleep thinking how much the nurse reminded her of her mother. The two women had that same caring attitude.

She woke a few hours later thinking about Monica and what she would say about all this, and her stomach clenched with tension. Her mother-in-law had flown south to stay at her sister's place in Alice Springs for a few days, so at least she had a reprieve until the next day when Monica was due to call. Then there would be hell to pay.

She mentioned it to Flynn when he came into her bedroom later that evening. "I'll have to tell Monica where I am," she said, once he'd finished inquiring if she felt better.

"*I'll* deal with Monica," he said, his tone telling her the issue wasn't open to negotiation.

"No." She had to stand her ground with him. "I'll speak to her."

"I won't have you getting upset."

Not for the first time today, she saw past his arrogance to his concern. It warmed her. "She needs to know, Flynn. And she needs to hear it from me."

"Then I insist on being with you when you tell her."

"Fine," she agreed, but if she could help it, she had no intention of letting him be around when she broke the news to Monica. Her mother-in-law was going to be very upset as it was.

"You didn't eat much dinner," he said, cutting across her thoughts, obviously having spoken to Jean.

"I wasn't really hungry." A light soup had been all she could manage.

"You've got to eat."

That's when she realized *he* looked tired. It had been a long day for him, too. "Have *you* eaten?"

He appeared surprised by her question. "No. I thought I'd dine in here and keep you company."

She moistened her lips. "Er…in here?"

"This is *our* bedroom, Danielle."

She swallowed as her heart started to beat fast. "I don't remember saying I would share a bedroom with you."

"I don't remember asking."

"Flynn, I—"

His gaze locked with hers. "We start as we intend to go on."

"All of a sudden it's *we?*" She could feel herself being suffocated. Just as Robert had smothered her.

"Forget about him," he said harshly, reading her thoughts.

She took a shaky breath. "I can't."

"Face the facts, Danielle. He only wanted you physically because he couldn't have you emotionally. *That's* why he wouldn't let you go."

She knew he was right but it still hurt to know she'd been used in such a way by the man who'd been her husband. "And your reasons are different?"

"My reasons are my own, but I'll tell you one thing. They're a damn sight more noble than his ever were." With that he stormed off into the bathroom.

Danielle bit her lip, then lay back against the pillows, knowing Flynn was right. Despite his arrogance, he had an honor code about him that Robert would never have understood. It gave her a strange comfort and seemed to fill an empty void inside her that had never been filled.

Not by Robert.

Nor Monica.

As for the older woman, Danielle had the opportunity to talk to her sooner rather than later when Monica rang while Flynn was eating dinner.

There was a knock at the bedroom door and Jean opened it at Flynn's command. "Excuse me, Mr. Donovan, I know you don't want Dani… I mean, Mrs. Ford to be disturbed, but there's a very irate lady on the telephone demanding that she speak with her." The nurse glanced at Danielle. "She said she's your mother-in-law."

Trepidation filled Danielle as she looked across the room at Flynn sitting at the small table near the window. "How does she know I'm here?"

"I had your phone calls forwarded," he said, giving no excuse for not mentioning it previously. He glanced back at the nurse. "Danielle will call her back tomorrow."

"But—"

"No," Danielle refuted. "I can't do that to her, Flynn. She'll worry herself sick all night."

"Better than her making *you* sick."

"But I'll worry all night, too." Danielle looked at Jean's concerned face. "I'll take the call."

The older woman hesitated, then nodded at the phone on the bedside table. "Line one," she said, and closed the door behind herself, leaving her and Flynn alone again.

Danielle glanced at the phone, then at Flynn. "I'd like some privacy please."

"I'm not leaving," he said, leaning back in the chair and picking up his wineglass.

"Flynn—"

"Monica's waiting," he pointed out, and took a sip of wine as he watched her through narrowed eyes. Danielle gritted her teeth, then reached for the phone.

She took a deep breath and lifted the receiver. "Monica, it's Danielle."

"Danielle?" the other woman said anxiously. "What's going on? I come back from my sister's early and call you at home and now I'm being put through to you at someone's house."

"Monica, I have something to tell you. I'm er… staying at a friend's house for a while."

A gasp came down the line. "A friend? What friend?"

As briefly as she could, Danielle explained about being kicked out of her apartment. She deliberately didn't say anything about feeling faint.

"Why are you staying there instead of with me?" Monica demanded, her voice turning colder. "This has something to do with that Flynn Donovan. I knew he was up to something when I met him. His eyes were all over you."

As they are now, Danielle thought, suppressing a shiver. "You're being ridiculous."

"Ridiculous, am I? I bet he's had you kicked out of your apartment so you would move in with him."

"That's not true. Flynn had nothing to do with me having to move." She saw his glance sharpen, but Monica soon demanded the attention back on her.

"Aah! So you *have* gone to live with him. Oh, my God."

"It's only for a short while," Danielle tried to placate. "Just until I find another apartment."

"He's brainwashed you, hasn't he?" And then the tears started and once again Danielle was thrown back into the past. The other woman wouldn't let up, wouldn't even listen. Danielle was in the middle of trying to speak when the phone was suddenly taken out of her hands.

Flynn spoke into the receiver. "Monica, this is Flynn Donovan. Danielle is staying here with me. Get over it." He hung up the phone, then stood looking down at her, his eyes banked with displeasure. "Don't let her manipulate you, Danielle."

She gasped with hurt. He knew what she'd been through yet he made it sound so easy. "Are you calling me weak willed?"

He sat down beside her, his hard mouth visibly relaxing. "Not at all. You're very strong willed, in fact. But you're just too nice to people at your own detriment." He reached out and touched her ear, his finger lightly tracing the shell-like feature. "Of course, I notice you don't seem to have a problem standing up to *me*." His finger stopped moving, his eyes trapped her. "Why?"

Her heart skipped a beat. "I don't like arrogant men."

"As opposed to self-centered, manipulative women like your mother-in-law?" he mocked, his finger on the move again, sliding along her chin toward her mouth.

He had a point, but that point was being reduced by his smooth touch. "You don't know what you're up against, Flynn," she said huskily.

"The only person I care to be up against is you, sweetheart," he murmured, his finger sliding onto her lower lip, stroking it. She was sinking fast. She knew it as well as he did.

"Flynn…" The tip of her tongue escaped to lick her suddenly dry lips, but instead brushed against his finger. She froze at the same time he did. His eyes darkened. He was going to kiss her.

But in one swift movement he pushed himself to his feet and stood looking down at her, his tension a tangible thing. "I want you again so much my gut aches," he said, his voice simmering with barely checked passion.

She couldn't look away.

Couldn't breathe.

She couldn't think past wanting him.

"But I can wait," he rasped, and strode out of the room.

An hour later, Danielle was flicking nervously through a magazine waiting for Flynn to return, when she heard voices coming from downstairs. Then one voice rose above the rest and her heart slammed against her ribs. Monica!

Swallowing hard, she slipped into her blue silk robe and hurried from the room, rushing to look over the balcony to the front entrance below. She stiffened in shock.

"I don't believe you," her mother-in-law was saying wildly to Flynn. "You've kidnapped her."

Flynn's hard gaze sliced through Monica. "Danielle hasn't been kidnapped. She's here of her own free will, though I doubt you understand that particular concept, Monica."

Her face twisted in anger. "You're a fine one to talk," she spat. "Danielle doesn't even like you. She told me so. She *hates* you. That's why I *know* you've kidnapped her."

Danielle had heard enough. She couldn't let this go any further. "Flynn is right," she said, walking down the sweeping staircase as they turned to look up at her. "I *am* here of my own free will."

"Danielle!" Monica rushed forward. "You don't have to say that just because he's here. I'll protect you."

Danielle reached the bottom of the stairs but she kept her distance from the other woman. "From what, Monica? Flynn has been nothing but kind to me." And when it came down to it, it was the truth of late. Her eyes told him so as she glanced at him and saw the encouragement in those dark depths. She felt an odd flutter in the region of her chest.

Monica paled. "You should have come home to me. I would have looked after you. It's not too late. Go get dressed and we can leave right now."

Danielle stood her ground. "There's no need."

Monica clutched at Danielle's wrist, as if she wanted to grab her and run out the door with her. "But can't you see he only wants one thing."

Danielle knew she couldn't deny that charge, but it wasn't what Monica thought. Flynn wanted marriage, not just sex out of her. Yet if she let her mother-in-law see she had hit a nerve, she would be lost.

Before she could say anything, Flynn stepped forward and extricated Monica's hand from Danielle's wrist. Danielle instinctively rubbed the tender skin, only now realizing how painful the other woman's grip had been. Then she felt Flynn's arm snake around her waist and pull her against him, hip to hip, providing a united front.

"The only thing I want from Danielle is for her to marry me," he said, his hand tightening when she froze, silently telling her to remain quiet.

Somehow she held back a groan of despair.

Monica inhaled sharply. "Marry you! You can't marry her. She's carrying my son's child."

"The baby is a part of Danielle and as my wife, he will be part of my life, too."

"You could never love another man's child," Monica choked.

"On the contrary."

Something happened to Danielle when she heard those words. She didn't know why, nor attempt to understand, but for the first time since her parents' death she felt warm from the inside out.

Monica flashed him a look of disdain. "You don't care about Danielle or the baby."

"*I'm* not the one upsetting her like this." Flynn's voice held an undertone of contempt.

As if she knew she was defeated, tears began to well in Monica's eyes. "Danielle, how can you do this to me? You know that baby is Robbie's."

Danielle's throat turned dry as the feeling of being smothered washed over her. Monica was being manipulative again but how could she *not* feel sorry for the other woman?

"Bloody hell," Flynn growled. "Get out of my house. I will not have you pulling these tricks on Danielle."

Monica's tears stopped as quickly as they started. "I told you to stay away from Danielle but you wouldn't listen, would you?" She hissed, but before Danielle could register the words fully, Monica turned on her and flushed an ugly look. "This is all *your* fault!"

The unfairness of the accusation made Danielle flinch inwardly, but in that instant she knew she'd finally had enough. She'd taken a stand against this woman over moving out of her house, but she now knew that had only been a token step. She had to stand up to Monica as a person in her own right. It was time to show her mother-in-law she would no longer be an extension of her dead husband.

"No, Monica. If it's anyone's fault, it's yours. You spoiled Robert so much you turned him into a brat who took everything he could from me."

Monica gasped. "You were his wife."

"I was his wife, not his slave to do what he wanted with me. I had rights, too."

For a split second it looked as if Monica would argue. She opened her mouth…. She tried to speak…. Then before their very eyes she began to crumple to the ground.

"He was my son," she wailed, falling on her knees. "My son! And now he's dead. What am I going to do?" She wept aloud, her sobs increasing with intensity.

The sound of her grief brought Jean running. The nurse immediately went to her aid. Louise and Thomas appeared, looking worried, and went to help Jean.

Danielle swallowed past the lump in her throat. No matter what had gone on between them, she felt for the other woman's heartache. It was deep and genuine. Just as Monica's love for her son was deep and genuine.

She went to move forward, too, but Flynn stopped her. "No. Let them handle this."

"But—"

"Jean's a professional, Danielle. Allow her to do her job."

He was right, so she let him walk her up the stairs. But she could feel his suppressed anger in every movement of his body. An anger that she knew was directed at Monica but made her shiver all the same. He looked hard and dangerous and ready to do someone harm. He would be a formidable enemy, this man. But then, she'd always known that.

He closed the bedroom door behind them and she walked across the plush carpet to the bed and sank down on the luxurious cover. A heavy silence filled the room.

Then some things fell into place for Danielle.

"Monica was the one who had me kicked out of the apartment, wasn't she?"

He inclined his head. "I believe so."

"And she warned you away from me, didn't she? You wanted to protect me from her."

He held her gaze. "Yes."

She swallowed, glad she now knew the reason for his proposal of marriage, yet oddly disappointed.

"But that's not the only reason," he added.

She sucked in a sharp breath even as her heart thudded against her ribs. "Um…it isn't?"

"I'm deeply attracted to you, Danielle. I want you as my wife. For me, not because of Monica. But if after the baby's born you still want to leave, I won't stop you."

At one time she would have told him to go to hell for being so manipulative, but now…after knowing he had tried to protect her…after hearing the way he'd spoken to Monica…she realized he did care for her.

Perhaps more than he wanted to.

"And I owe you an apology for something else," he said without inflection, but the tautened skin of his cheekbones belied the deceptively quiet statement.

A crease formed between her brows. "You do?"

A muscle ticked in his cheek. "Seeing Monica in action just now and the way she used everything in the book to emotionally blackmail you, I finally understood why you so badly crave your independence."

Emotion welled in her throat as the tension eased inside her. Having Flynn fully appreciate what she'd gone through meant so much.

"And I suspect this is just the tip of the iceberg, right?"

For several more seconds he held her gaze. She wanted to look away but couldn't. "Yes," she admitted.

His eyes glittered with something so strong, so palpable, she felt a shiver roll down her spine. "Tell me about your marriage."

She drew a calming breath, glad to be able to talk about it. "It was a mistake almost from the start, but I tried to pretend it didn't matter. After a while I couldn't even do that anymore."

"Did you love him?"

"I thought I did, but I soon found out his idea of marriage was different than mine. He wanted unconditional love and I…well, I just wanted to be free."

"Yet you fell pregnant to him," he pointed out, his eyes detached but she knew he wasn't.

"Not on purpose, Flynn. I would never have wanted my child to be brought up in that sort of atmosphere." She took a shaky breath, trying to ignore the sick feeling in her stomach at the thought. "No, it just happened. I was finally ready to leave Robert, but he convinced me not to walk out on our marriage and to give it one more try. I knew I didn't love him anymore. I knew he was probably being manipulative but…" She swallowed hard. "He said things would be different from now on, only he never got the chance to prove it. He was killed in a car accident a week later."

Slowly Flynn's shoulders looked less tense. "I'm sorry for what he did to you. For what they *both* did to you. If I could take away your pain, I would."

Sudden tears sprang to her eyes. No matter what had passed between her and Flynn, no matter how angry he'd made her feel, or what accusations he'd thrown at her or how arrogant he'd become, he'd given her so much.

"You already have," she murmured, blinking back her tears. "Oh, Flynn, when we made love, you made me feel like a woman again, instead of a poor example of a wife."

His dark eyes deepened in color. "You would never be a poor example of anything. Never."

She swallowed hard. "Thank you."

Just then the wail of a siren could be heard coming closer, and the real world intruded. She saw a shutter come down over Flynn's face.

He reached for the door handle. "Rest now. I'll see to this." He opened the door then looked back at her, his eyes bleak. "I'll be moving into the bedroom next door. You need have no fear of being smothered by me any longer."

"Oh, but…" His words clutched at her heart, making her aware that she suddenly didn't like this wall he was putting between them. "Flynn, I don't want you to use another bedroom. I want you to share my bed. I—" it was hard for her to say this "—need you right now."

He froze, his dark eyes riveting on her face. "Are you sure?"

"Yes." She moistened her lips. "So…will you be coming back?"

His eyes searched hers, reading her thoughts. "You can count on it," he said brusquely, then left the room.

She sat there for long moments after he'd gone, exhausted but incredibly relieved by his words. No matter how apprehensive she was about their relationship, no matter that it had progressed to another deeper level, it was somehow important to have Flynn by her side, if only until the baby was born.

After the ambulance left, Flynn went into the study, reached for one of the unopened bottles on the bar and poured himself a large measure of whiskey. It should have burned going down but it didn't. He was already burning inside. Burning to take a certain dead man by the throat and rip his heart out.

And Monica. She was certainly a piece of work. She'd admitted having her daughter-in-law kicked out of the penthouse and then tried to dump everything on Danielle's slim shoulders. It was just as well the older woman was on her way to a psychiatric hospital. She needed help and he doubted she would be released for quite some time.

Danielle must have gone through a living hell with those two. The thought of it appalled him.

But what appalled him even more was that *he* had been doing the same thing to her, telling her what to do and smothering her independence just as surely as Robert and Monica had done, not to mention accusing her of all sorts of things she *hadn't* done.

He'd found that out after Connie had called a half hour ago with the report he'd ordered on Danielle and Robert Ford. She'd unearthed the personal information that had made him feel sick at heart.

He now knew *all* his accusations had been unfounded. Danielle wasn't a gold digger. And she hadn't spent the money from the loan. And the penthouse hadn't been offered to her by an ex-lover. Nor had she wasted her husband's inheritance and frittered away a fortune of his money. The looking to buy a secondhand car for her and the baby had been genuine.

She deserved a medal for what he'd put her through.

Yet she forgave him.

And she still wanted him in her life.

He swallowed another measure of whiskey. It had taken a blond-haired, blue-eyed temptress to remind him that the world did not exist for the sheer pleasure of Flynn Donovan. He felt humble and that was a feeling he hadn't felt in a long, long time.

Nine

The next morning Danielle woke to find herself in Flynn's arms, her back up against him. Last night he'd come to bed, pulled her into his arms and explored her mouth with his tongue, stamping her with his kiss. Then he'd growled, "Get some rest," rolled over and slept with his back to her.

She'd lain there, aching for him, knowing he was awake, knowing he was wanting her as much as she wanted him, but aware he was thinking of her health. Yet she'd merely have to reach out and touch him to change all that, only she couldn't quite bring herself to do it. It was as if she'd made the first move, she would have been truly lost.

But that didn't stop her from giving a little sigh and

moving her buttocks against him now, then freezing when she felt his arousal.

"It's no use pretending," he murmured, his face buried against her nape.

"Er…pretending?"

"That you're not awake."

She released a breath. "Who said I was pretending?"

He went up on one elbow and rolled her onto her back. "Awake or not, you won't stop me wanting you."

"What *will* stop you wanting me?" she said, her voice husky.

"Nothing," he muttered. "Not a bloody thing."

"Oh, Flynn," she whispered.

His eyes filled with a hot, sensual look that made the very air pulse with desire. "Say my name like that again and I'll just have to make love to you."

Her bones melted at those words, at that look, and all rational thought went with them. She moistened her lips. "And I have no say in the matter?"

"None at all." A predatory gleam entered his eyes, then his gaze slid downward, pausing a moment on the swell of her breasts under her cream nightgown before they returned to rest on her heated face. "Your body wants me to make love to you."

She tried to hold back a moan but somehow it escaped, making his eyes darken, making him look even more devastatingly attractive. And dangerous.

"If I don't have you soon, there'll be hell to pay," he growled, lowering his lips to her bare shoulder beneath the spaghetti straps, making her jump. He inhaled deeply. "You're wearing the perfume I gave you." And then he began grazing his way along her collarbone, up the column of her throat, along her chin. "I'm going to kiss you now."

Suddenly she had no will of her own and her lips parted ever so slightly. His mouth took possession of hers, and she shuddered with pleasure, her defenses downing as if they were bowing to a master craftsman. Everything inside her welcomed him as she responded to each plunge of his tongue across hers. She quivered and slid her hands up to his shoulders, holding on to him in case this turned into a dream and he suddenly disappeared.

He broke off the kiss, breathing heavily, his eyes smoldering for her, the intensity in them making her heart thud against her chest. Something had strengthened between them that went beyond sexual desire.

And then with great care he stripped the nightgown from her body, kissing every inch of bare skin as it was exposed to his view. Tears stung her eyes at the precious way he made love to her.

"Danielle?" he growled, lifting his head from the slope of her breast.

She blinked back the tears. "Yes?"

"Are you okay?"

"Please don't stop. This is so…wonderful."

He gave an almost feral groan. "I have no intention of stopping," he said, then kissed her hard on the mouth. "Enough talk. Let's enjoy each other."

She couldn't have spoken anyway because after that he set her blood on fire, scorching her with a passion that set her *world* on fire. And when he was inside her, she tried to ignore the possessive glitter in his eyes that said *this time* he'd made her his own.

Two weeks later, Flynn had to go to Brisbane on business for a couple of days and Danielle soon found she missed him. Nothing was the same without him. Yesterday had seemed duller and longer. The house seemed empty, the bed big and lonely.

She tried to tell herself it was just as well, that eventually she'd have to get used to not having him in her life again, only she couldn't summon the energy. It was as if she were running low on batteries and she needed Flynn to recharge her.

"You miss him, don't you?" Louise said as she served Danielle a late dinner on the patio, the dazzling sunset casting a golden hue over the landscaped swimming pool and cascading waterfall.

"He's only been gone one night," Danielle teased.

Louise sent her a wry look. "You're fooling yourself, you know."

Danielle's cheeks reddened. "Flynn—"

"Needs you. And the baby. I can see how happy you make him, Danielle, and that makes me happy. I remember him as a child and he was a very sad little boy."

Danielle's heart squeezed tight at the thought of Flynn's childhood. She could just picture him as a dark-haired boy picking up after his drunken father, making them something for dinner, from the meager scraps in the cupboard, his clothes threadbare.

"Why didn't anyone help him back then, Louise? He was so young."

"We all tried, but his father was a proud man and wouldn't accept help and somehow the authorities never seemed to take any action."

How could any parent make their own children suffer in such a fashion? In *any* fashion?

"How did his mother die?"

"In childbirth."

Danielle gasped. "Flynn's mother died having a baby?"

"Yes, but it won't happen to you," Louise quickly assured her. "She died a long time ago. They have much better medical treatments now."

Danielle sat there, stunned. And he hadn't told her? For a moment an incredible hurt clutched at her throat.

Then she realized that perhaps he *had* told her, but not in words. There had been his seeming anger when he'd found out she was pregnant and living alone. He'd stayed away from her, not because he'd thought she was trying to trap him as she'd suspected, but because the child she carried was a painful reminder of how his mother had died. An agony he didn't want to deal with every day.

Yet here they were now.

"You love him, Danielle," Louise said, interrupting her thoughts. "I know you do. I can see it in your eyes every time you say his name."

Danielle blinked. "That's ridiculous. You've got it all wrong."

"No, I haven't." With that, Louise picked up an empty dish from the table and went back in the house.

Danielle sat back in her chair and stared after her. Louise was wrong. So totally wrong. She didn't love Flynn. She wouldn't let herself fall in love again, no matter how attracted she was to the man. She was stronger than that. Stronger and…a fool.

A fool in love.

Something unfurled inside her, came full circle and completed what had begun the day she'd met Flynn. Louise was right. She loved him. The thought staggered her, sent her reeling. Thank goodness she was sitting down.

She loved Flynn Donovan.

Oh, my God! She'd been too blind to see it before. Or maybe she just hadn't wanted to know. Because loving Flynn meant making a commitment. And commitment meant something inside her had changed.

But had she changed enough to lay everything on the line and marry him? Certainly if he learned to love her, too, the rewards would be great. But if it all went wrong? The pain would be unbearable.

She swallowed hard. Could she marry a man who may only lust after her for the next twenty years…if that long? Dear God, she just didn't know.

Suddenly her skin prickled and her heart began thudding in her chest. Her gaze shot to the patio door. Flynn stood there, his look so captivating in the fading light it sent a tremor through her.

"Flynn!"

In one fluid movement, he came toward her, tilted up her head and kissed her with a thoroughness that made her heart roll over. She melted into him, letting him take her lips as an offering of her love.

"You're pleased to see me," he murmured, easing back, a purely masculine look of satisfaction in his eyes.

She tried to act nonchalant. She needed more time. "I was bored. You break the monotony."

The corner of his mouth quirked upward as he straightened. "I'm glad I'm useful for something."

She moistened her lips. "Have you fixed the problem at the Brisbane office already?"

"No. I fly back first thing in the morning."

She frowned. "So why are you here?"

His gaze held hers. "I wanted to see you."

For a heart-stopping moment she savored the words. Then she released a slow breath. "Thank you for your concern, but I'm fine."

His expression held a note of mockery but before she could catch her breath, his eyes turned probing. "Tell me. Do you still think I smother you?"

All at once she realized something. His concern wasn't about stifling her. It was about *caring* for her. And he wasn't someone who wanted to control her for his own purposes, but someone who wanted to protect her because he genuinely had her welfare at heart.

No wonder she had fallen in love with him.

Her throat closed up and it took a moment to speak. "No, I don't feel smothered by you. Not any-more."

His eyes darkened. "I'm glad." Then he turned to face the pool and, if she didn't know better, she'd have said his movements were somewhat jerky. Because of her? Or slight jetlag?

"I could do with a swim," he said, loosening his tie. "Want to join me?"

The thought was far too tempting, but she didn't

know if she'd be able to control her words if she was in his arms right now. She might blurt out she loved him.

"Er…no. I've already been for a dip today." She watched as he started stripping off his suit. "Um…what are you doing?"

He gave a half-smile, full of confidence again. "Taking off my clothes."

Heaven help her. "But Louise?"

"Is in the kitchen making me dinner. Don't worry. I'll leave my underpants on. I'd hate to shock her." But his eyes said he knew it wasn't just Louise he wanted to shock.

As if mesmerized, Danielle watched as he stripped, then walked over to the pool, the garden lights having turned on automatically as dusk descended, the palm trees and ferns almost hugging him as he stepped onto the edge.

He stood there for a moment, looking down at the crystal clear water, his tight black underpants leaving little to her imagination as the underwater lights reflected his superb physique, all sinew and muscle, giving him a commanding air of self-confidence.

He plunged into the water as he had plunged into her heart, surfaced, then began to swim up and down the pool with long, powerful strokes that sliced through the water as he sliced through life, determined to thrust through any obstacle in his way to get to where he wanted.

Or to *what* he wanted.

He wanted *her.*

He'd told her so with words, with his eyes, with his actions. The thought both thrilled and frightened her, because now she knew his wanting her made her stronger, not weaker. To belong to Flynn in the truest sense of the word would be wonderful.

She swallowed. Oh, God. She wasn't ready for all these feelings overwhelming her. She had to think.

Pushing herself to her feet, she ignored the ache in her back and went into the kitchen, hanging around while Louise prepared steak and salad for his dinner. She could feel Louise's knowing eyes on her while Thomas chatted on about their nephew's new job.

Ten minutes later Flynn strolled into the kitchen and fell into conversation with the older couple. He'd wrapped a white towel around his lean hips, his tanned skin beaded with water. Danielle wanted to lick every drop off him, smooth her palms over the dark springy hair on his chest, rip that towel away and touch lower.

Make love to him.

She gave a silent moan and made for the door, intent on going up to the bedroom, putting some space between them.

He stepped in front of her, stopping her from leaving. "Come talk to me while I eat dinner."

Her eyes darted down to his broad chest. Big mistake. They darted up again. "I think I'll call it an early night."

His lingering gaze sent warmth creeping up her neck. "Then I'll join you later," he murmured, and stepped aside for her to leave.

Swallowing, she said good-night to the older couple and forced her legs to walk out of that room. She doubted she would sleep. Not when she wanted Flynn with every breath in her body.

* * *

Flynn scowled as he watched Danielle leave the kitchen. She was very beautiful and very pregnant now, but there was something different about her tonight. She seemed more on edge.

About the baby? Perhaps.

About each other? Definitely.

He swallowed tightly. He'd missed her last night. Nothing had seemed the same without Danielle in bed with him. He'd become used to her soft skin against his own. Her scent. Her quiet breathing. And, yes, her frequent trips to the bathroom.

He hadn't felt right when they weren't even in the same city. Hell, make that the same room. Without her beside him it was as if something vital was missing. It was the reason he'd arranged for his jet to bring him home tonight. He couldn't spend another night without her next to him.

But despite a strong urge to go to her now, he had to attend to some urgent business calls first.

It ended up being late by the time Flynn got to bed, so he showered in one of the spare bathrooms so as not to wake Danielle, then made his way to their bedroom. He crossed in the moonlight to the other side of the bed, quietly sliding in next to her.

She lay sleeping on her side facing away from him and he closed in on her but didn't touch. He wanted to pull her around to face him, but she was sleeping heavily and didn't have the heart to wake her.

Instead, he lay there for ages, breathing in her special fragrance. His gut ached to make her his own, yet oddly it was enough just to lie next to her, knowing there was no place else on earth he'd rather be. Eventually he fell asleep from sheer exhaustion.

And was awoken in the early hours by her cheek rubbing against his chest. He froze as he lay on his back. She had burrowed up against him, her soft breath sighing over his skin.

"Flynn?" she murmured half-asleep.

"It had better be," he muttered, his arms tightening around her. Just having her ask if it was him beside her made him want to possess her until she never asked again. He wanted no other man in her mind. No other man belonged there but *him*.

When he knew she had fully woken, his blood heated, ready to flow over her, merge with her, storm her if necessary.

A moment crept by and from out of nowhere she placed her lips against his chest and kissed him there. He sucked in air, then growled, "Danielle?"

"It had better be," she mimicked huskily, the caress of her fingers on his chest putting him on full alert. Her satin-covered breasts pressed against his arm as her fingers trailed down the center of his chest. In the moonlight streaming across their bed, he saw her smile.

Then her fingers slid across his abdomen and curled around his straining erection. He gave a moan from deep in his throat. He'd wanted her to initiate their lovemaking for a while now…to touch him first and not the other way around. Yes, she'd always welcomed him and responded to his passion, but that initial touch…that initial wanting…had always been his.

Until now.

"Are you sure?" he rasped, barely able to say the words but managing it all the same.

"Yes." She kissed him briefly on the lips. "Now lie back and enjoy this. Let me pleasure *you*," she said, sliding her hand along him, arousing him even more.

With a rough moan of surrender, he gave in.

Surprisingly, for all her insistence, she wasn't quite as sure in her movements, telling him she hadn't done this particular aspect of lovemaking before. A triumphant heat ran through him before he took charge, his hand over hers, guiding her, showing her what he liked and how he liked it. Together they stroked him, first with long slow movements, then picking up speed.

She grew more confident, so he removed his hand and let her fly solo. Only, there was nothing solo about this experience. She watched him as she caressed him, her eyes turning darker, smokier, with each passing second.

Awareness shot through him. Other women had pleasured him this way, skillfully using their hands and mouth to give him satisfaction. But this woman, with hands not quite so skillful, her delicious mouth not nearly close enough to his, gave him the most erotic experience of his life. It was the look in her eyes that did it, her pleasure in watching him.

When he finally finished shuddering, he rolled away for a moment. Then he spun back and faced her, giving her a long kiss. "Thank you."

She offered him a slumberous smile. "No, thank *you*."

He traced her lower lip with his finger. "You'll pay

for this," he teased, intending to take his time in pleasuring her.

"Oh, I hope so," she whispered, then rested her cheek against his chest and lowered her lashes, but not before he saw a strange look in her eyes, making his heart stop beating for a second.

But before he could wonder about that look, she murmured, "I'm sleepy now, Flynn."

He watched her eyes close fully and he took a breath, tenderly kissing her silky hair, holding her close until her body relaxed fully in sleep against him.

Yet the look she'd given had him thinking. He rarely second-guessed himself, but there'd been something different about that look. And his insides screamed she was holding something back.

Ten

Over the next few weeks as her baby grew inside her, Danielle found their relationship had moved to another level. For some reason Flynn had changed. He didn't seem quite as hard or alone as he'd been before.

She knew she had changed, as well. How could she not? Thankfully her pregnancy was making her increasingly mellow and she was grateful, now, that Flynn had asked her to come here to live. Loving him would one day break her heart, but that was in the future. She felt more at peace with herself than she'd felt in a long time.

Of course, loving him also meant she found it harder to erect her usual barriers against him. Lord knows she tried to keep an emotional distance when he suggested she redecorate the dining room then encouraged her to do the rest of the house, or came to her birthing classes, or even when he asked her over dinner how her day had been.

Then she'd see him watching her with a glittering light in his eyes that said he wanted her…and would go on wanting her and when he'd take her in his arms later that night she'd melt for him. She'd forget for the moment that after the baby was born, she'd need to walk away from the man she loved.

Her dreams usually reflected her thoughts, and more so now because of her pregnancy. So it was no surprise when Danielle had a dream she was swimming in the warm ocean. She felt buoyant and alive as she lay on her back, looking up at the bright blue sky, Flynn beside her.

And then the dream changed. The water had turned cold and her stomach had begun to cramp. She was beginning to sink. She reached out for Flynn but he wasn't there.

She woke with a start and realized the pain in her stomach was real, and her heart jumped in her throat as she lifted the quilt, relieved when everything seemed fine.

Then another cramp hit, making her gasp. Dear God. *The baby.*

Panic filled her and suddenly she wanted Flynn by her side. Her first instinct was to call him at work. She reached for the phone, but her hand stopped midair. He'd said he had an important meeting today. Should she interrupt him?

Then something struck her. Could she really ask this

of him now that she knew of his past? Hadn't he suffered enough from the scars of his mother's death? Could she put him through a possible miscarriage?

She almost cried at that last thought, and her hand dropped to her side. If she lost the baby...if it was going to happen...and, dear God, she hoped it didn't...she couldn't do this to Flynn. Not to the man she loved.

She'd go to the hospital first and take it from there. Perhaps she was overreacting. If everything was okay, she'd even call him from the hospital and tell him about it then.

She would go to the hospital, she decided, pushing herself out of bed, her knees shaky. The pain was low in her abdomen but she could still walk okay. She dressed and phoned down to Thomas, asking him to bring the car around as she had suddenly remembered a doctor's appointment at the hospital.

Louise was a bit harder to convince, her sharp eyes watching as Danielle told the housekeeper she didn't want any breakfast.

"You should eat something," the older woman insisted.

"I don't have time, Louise," she said, and walked out to the car as carefully as she could.

Thomas helped her into the Mercedes and she schooled her features as she felt her stomach cramp again. Thank goodness the hospital was only ten minutes away.

"My God!" Flynn whispered, a white mist seeming to cover his eyes, blocking his vision. He couldn't believe what Louise was telling him on the telephone.

Danielle had started having pains and had gone to the hospital without telling him.

"She didn't look herself when she came downstairs this morning," Louise continued. "And then I got suspicious when she said she had a doctor's appointment and I knew she didn't. So after Thomas dropped her off, I told him to take me to her."

"Don't leave her side," he ordered.

"Flynn, the doctor said she was going to be okay," she assured him quickly.

"I'll be there soon," he managed to say, not daring to believe that. He dropped the telephone back in place, then strode out the office door, throwing out instructions to Connie to get his car *now*.

How could Danielle even think about *not* telling him? Did she think he cared so little about her and the baby? Didn't she know he loved her?

It hit him then. They belonged together. She was his, and he was hers.

He loved her.

He swallowed hard and tried not to think about losing her. Losing them both. *Dear God, please don't take them away from me.* He couldn't imagine a life without her now. Danielle filled every crevice, every pore, every beat of his heart.

By the time he arrived at the hospital, he'd been to hell and back. He didn't even see Louise get up and leave as he entered the room. He had eyes only for Danielle, whose face had lit up when she saw him, sending a jolt of love through his chest.

"Flynn, everything's fine," Danielle said hurriedly as

he strode toward her. "The doctor did some tests and they're all normal."

An avalanche of relief swept over him…through him… Danielle and the baby were going to be okay.

He kissed her hard, then pulled back with a rough groan. "You should have told me," he rasped. "I wanted to be with you."

Her eyes softened as she reached out and touched his face. "I know how your mother died, Flynn. Louise told me."

He swore. So that was what this was all about. "She's fired."

"Don't be mad at Louise. She *did* tell you I was here, didn't she?"

Okay, so maybe he wouldn't fire her. Louise loved Danielle anyway. How could she not?

He brought her hand to his lips. "I love you, Danielle. I love you with everything in me. With all my heart."

Her lips parted on a gasp. "You do?"

He took a breath, stared intently into her eyes and thanked God he had a second chance to say what he was feeling to the woman he loved. "I want you, my love. And I want to be inside you. Not just with my body but with my heart. You are part of me."

A whirlwind of emotions flickered over her face, then settled to just one. "I love you, Flynn Donovan. You're everything I want in a man. You're good and kind and decent and you've lifted the darkness from my heart. I want to spend the rest of my life with you."

Flynn's heart expanded, stunned by the sheer look of love shining from her eyes. It wrapped around him, flowed through him, became one with him. He had to have her in his life. It was that simple.

He kissed her again, lingered, then shaped her face with his hands. "You already knew you loved me, didn't you?"

Soft pink entered her cheeks. "Yes. It was the time you came back from Brisbane just to be with me."

He remembered that night well. It had been the first time she'd initiated their lovemaking, when he'd felt she'd kept something back. Now he knew what that something was.

"Will you marry me?"

Her eyes shone. "Oh, yes."

"That's what I like to hear." Then he realized what he'd said and he winced. "I'll try not to smother you. I'll let you have time to yourself. You'd be a wonderful interior designer and I think you should do some training. You'll do well and—"

"Thank you for that," she said, reaching out and stroking his chin. "As long as you love me I'll be happy, my darling."

He kissed her mouth again, believing her, believing *in* her. "If my love is all it takes, then you're going to be one very pleased lady.

Epilogue

Danielle sucked in a sharp breath. "Oh. Here comes another one."

"Do your breathing exercises, sweetheart," Flynn coaxed.

A few minutes later, she relaxed back against the pillows, perspiration moistening her top lip. "That one's over." She looked at Flynn and sympathy filled her eyes. "You really don't have to stay with me. I'm fine."

He muttered a swearword under his breath. "I'm staying."

A worried frown marred her forehead. "It might get stressful," she warned.

He swallowed hard. "Do you know how stressed I already am?"

A soft curve touched her lips. "No. Tell me."

He caught her hand, kissed the inside of her wrist. "Temptress."

She smiled with love. Ever since their marriage three months ago, every day had been more than wonderful. She couldn't have asked for a more loving husband, nor for a better family and friends in Louise and Thomas, and in Flynn's friends, Kia, Brant and Damien.

She gasped. "Flynn, I need to speak to the nurse," she said as another contraction took hold.

"Where's the bloody doctor?" he growled, and strode to the door, looking up and down the hallway. "He should be here by now. I'm paying him enough."

As the contraction subsided, Danielle began to focus on her surroundings again. She looked at him and saw he was white around the mouth. Poor Flynn. He wasn't used to not being in control.

Another contraction hit. "Ooh, here comes another one. I think it's time to have the baby. I've got the urge to push. And it's gett-ing stron-ger," she panted.

He wiped her brow with a damp cloth. "Is there anything I can do?"

She grasped his hand and squeezed. "Just be with me."

He pushed the hair out of her eyes. "I'll be here, my love."

His words helped on one level, but not on another when the next contraction was fast rolling into the last one. They were coming so close together. She couldn't stop a moan of pain.

The next minute the medical staff arrived. "I don't think your baby's going to wait any longer," the doctor said after examining her.

The birth of her child began in earnest and everything became a blur. Contraction after contraction, the urge to push so strong that nothing could stop her now.

Flynn was by her side, encouraging her as the baby's head emerged.

He was there as her child slipped into the world.

And he was there by her side as the doctor announced it was a girl and she heard her daughter cry for the first time.

She cried as she cuddled her baby with love and wonder and looked up at Flynn, who kissed her gently on the lips.

"Well done, sweetheart," he murmured, his eyes bathing her in admiration. He looked so proud as he tenderly kissed the top of the baby's head. "She's perfect. Just like her mother."

Danielle's breath hitched in her throat. If anyone was perfect, it was this man she loved.

"Here," one of the nurses said. "Let me take the baby for a minute so I can clean her up." Before Danielle knew it, the woman had whisked her daughter to the corner of the room. "What are you going to call her?" the nurse asked over her shoulder.

Danielle had thought about names of course, but until now hadn't picked one out. But as she looked at Flynn, she knew. He'd been there for her throughout her pregnancy. He'd been here for her today. He may not be the father of her child, but he came, oh, so close.

"Alexandra," she said softly, seeing him give a start at the mention of his mother's name. "Yes, our baby's name will be Alexandra. Just like her grandmother."

For a moment Flynn looked stunned, then he leaned down and kissed her on the corner of her mouth. "Thank you," he whispered, the moisture in his eyes making her eyes glisten, too. They looked at each other for the longest moment.

But soon they were interrupted by other more important things and before too long, Danielle had been moved to a bed in a private room. Then they brought the baby in and suddenly the three of them were alone.

She took a shuddering breath. It was time to face Flynn and their future, but she had one more thing to do first. It was time to let go of the past.

She looked down at the baby in her arms and a swell of motherly love filled her. She kissed her baby's cheek, ruffled her fingers through the soft fuzz on her head.

"Sweetheart?" Flynn murmured.

She glanced up at him with tears in her eyes. Tears of joy. "Oh, Flynn, I was so afraid about having her. I thought deep down I might resent her because I didn't love Robert when we conceived her. I thought I might not love my baby in the way she should be loved." She gave a shaky smile. "But the love's there. She's in my heart."

Flynn's eyes brimmed with tenderness. "Has anyone ever told you what a beautiful person you are?"

She blinked back the tears, wanting to see this man she loved without hindrance. "No, not recently."

"Then let me do the honors, my love." Careful of the baby in her arms, he leaned forward and kissed her on the mouth. Softly. Gently. Wondrously. "You're a beautiful person, Danielle Donovan."

"Oh, Flynn," she whispered. "You always make me *feel* beautiful."

He kissed her again briefly. "I love you, sweetheart. You and little Alexandra and the other babies we will have."

Her heart turned over with love. "Others?" she teased.

"Not too many." He gently took the baby out of her arms, kissed Alexandra's forehead and placed her in the crib next to the bed.

Then he returned to Danielle, as he always would. "I want you to myself sometimes. No, I want you to myself *all* the time, but I'm willing to compromise. We'll get a nanny."

"I rather think Louise and Thomas might want to take on that job." Her smiled faded, her face growing serious. "Thank you for not giving up on me, Flynn. And for loving me unconditionally. And my daughter."

"*Our* daughter."

"Our daughter," she repeated as he lowered his head.

It was a long time before either of them came up for air. And that was just fine with Flynn. He rather liked being held captive by this woman who held his heart in her hands.

* * * * *

Don't miss the last of Maxine's millionaires in
THE EXECUTIVE'S VENGEFUL SEDUCTION

Mediterranean Nights

Join the guests and crew of Alexandra's Dream,
*the newest luxury ship to set sail on the
romantic Mediterranean, as they experience
the glamorous world of cruising.*

*A new Harlequin continuity series
begins in June 2007 with
FROM RUSSIA, WITH LOVE
by Ingrid Weaver*

*Marina Artamova books a cabin on the luxurious
cruise ship* Alexandra's Dream, *when she finds out
that her orphaned nephew and his adoptive father are
aboard. She's determined to be reunited with the
boy…but the romantic ambience of the ship and her
undeniable attraction to a man she considers her
enemy are about to interfere with her quest!*

Turn the page for a sneak preview!

Piraeus, Greece

"THERE SHE IS, Stefan. *Alexandra's Dream*." David Anderson squatted beside his new son and pointed at the dark blue hull that towered above the pier. The cruise ship was a majestic sight, twelve decks high and as long as a city block. A circle of silver and gold stars, the logo of the Liberty cruise line, gleamed from the swept-back smokestack. Like some legendary sea creature born for the water, the ship emanated power from every sleek curve—even at rest it held the promise of motion. "That's going to be our home for the next ten days."

The child beside him remained silent, his cheeks working in and out as he sucked furiously on his thumb.

Hair so blond it appeared white ruffled against his forehead in the harbor breeze. The baby-sweet scent unique
to the very young mingled with the tang of the sea.

"Ship," David said. "Uh, *parakhod.*"

From beneath his bangs, Stefan looked at the
Alexandra's Dream. Although he didn't release his
thumb, the corners of his mouth tightened with the beginning of a smile.

David grinned. That was Stefan's first smile this afternoon, one of only two since they had left the orphanage yesterday. It was probably because of the boat—
according to the orphanage staff, the boy loved boats,
which was the main reason David had decided to book
this cruise. Then again, there was a strong possibility
the smile could have been a reaction to David's attempt
at pocket-dictionary Russian. Whatever the cause, it
was a good start.

The liaison from the adoption agency had claimed
that Stefan had been taught some English, but David
had yet to see evidence of it. David continued to speak,
positive his son would understand his tone even if he
couldn't grasp the words. "This is her maiden voyage.
Her first trip, just like this is our first trip, and that
makes it special." He motioned toward the stage that
had been set up on the pier beneath the ship's bow.
"That's why everyone's celebrating."

The ship's official christening ceremony had been
held the day before and had been a closed affair, with
only the cruise-line executives and VIP guests invited,
but the stage hadn't yet been disassembled. Banners
bearing the blue and white of the Greek flag of the

ship's owner, as well as the Liberty circle of stars logo, draped the edges of the platform. In the center, a group of musicians and a dance troupe dressed in traditional white folk costumes performed for the benefit of the *Alexandra's Dream*'s first passengers. Their audience was in a festive mood, snapping their fingers in time to the music while the dancers twirled and wove through their steps.

David bobbed his head to the rhythm of the mandolins. They were playing a folk tune that seemed vaguely familiar, possibly from a movie he'd seen. He hummed a few notes. "Catchy melody, isn't it?"

Stefan turned his gaze on David. His eyes were a striking shade of blue, as cool and pale as a winter horizon and far too solemn for a child not yet five. Still, the smile that hovered at the corners of his mouth persisted. He moved his head with the music, mirroring David's motion.

David gave a silent cheer at the interaction. Hopefully, this cruise would provide countless opportunities for more. "Hey, good for you," he said. "Do you like the music?"

The child's eyes sparked. He withdrew his thumb with a pop. *"Moozika!"*

"Music. Right!" David held out his hand. "Come on, let's go closer so we can watch the dancers."

Stefan grasped David's hand quickly, as if he feared it would be withdrawn. In an instant his budding smile was replaced by a look close to panic.

Did he remember the car accident that had killed his parents? It would be a mercy if he didn't. As far as

David knew, Stefan had never spoken of it to anyone. Whatever he had seen had made him run so far from the crash that the police hadn't found him until the next day. The event had traumatized him to the extent that he hadn't uttered a word until his fifth week at the orphanage. Even now he seldom talked.

David sat back on his heels and brushed the hair from Stefan's forehead. That solemn, too-old gaze locked with his and, for an instant, David felt as if he looked back in time at an image of himself thirty years ago.

He didn't need to speak the same language to understand exactly how this boy felt. He knew what it meant to be alone and powerless among strangers, trying to be brave and tough but wishing with every fiber of his being for a place to belong, to be safe and, most of all, for someone to love him....

He knew in his heart he would be a good parent to Stefan. It was why he had never considered halting the adoption process after Ellie had left him. He hadn't balked when he'd learned of the recent claim by Stefan's spinster aunt, either; the absentee relative had shown up too late for her case to be considered. The adoption was meant to be. He and this child already shared a bond that went deeper than paperwork or legalities.

A seagull screeched overhead, making Stefan start and press closer to David.

"That's my boy," David murmured. He swallowed hard, struck by the simple truth of what he had just said.

That's my *boy.*

"I CAN'T BE PATIENT, RUDOLPH. I'm not going to stand by and watch my nephew get ripped from his country and his roots to live on the other side of the world."

Rudolph hissed out a slow breath. "Marina, I don't like the sound of that. What are you planning?"

"I'm going to talk some sense into this American kidnapper."

"No. Absolutely not. No offence, but diplomacy is not your strong suit."

"Diplomacy be damned. Their ship's due to sail at five o'clock."

"Then you wouldn't have an opportunity to speak with him even if his lawyer agreed to a meeting."

"I'll have ten days of opportunities, Rudolph, since I plan to be on board that ship."

* * * * *

Follow Marina and David as they join forces to uncover the reason behind little Stefan's unusual silence, and the secret behind the death of his parents....

Look for FROM RUSSIA, WITH LOVE by Ingrid Weaver in stores June 2007.

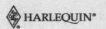

HARLEQUIN®

Mediterranean
NIGHTS™

Tycoon Elias Stamos is launching his newest luxury cruise ship from his home port in Greece. But someone from his past is eager to expose old secrets and to see the Stamos empire crumble.

Mediterranean Nights
launches in June 2007 with...

FROM RUSSIA, WITH LOVE
by *Ingrid Weaver*

Join the guests and crew of *Alexandra's Dream* as they are drawn into a world of glamour, romance and intrigue in this new 12-book series.

HARLEQUIN®
Super Romance®

Acclaimed author
Brenda Novak
returns to Dundee, Idaho, with

COULDA BEEN A COWBOY

After gaining custody of his infant son,
professional athlete Tyson Garnier hopes to escape
the media and find some privacy in Dundee, Idaho.
He also finds Dakota Brown. But is she ready for the
potential drama that comes with him?

Also watch for:

BLAME IT ON THE DOG by Amy Frazier
(Singles...with Kids)

HIS PERFECT WOMAN by Kay Stockham

DAD FOR LIFE by Helen Brenna
(A Little Secret)

MR. IRRESISTIBLE by Karina Bliss

WANTED MAN by Ellen K. Hartman

Available June 2007 wherever Harlequin books are sold!

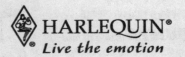

HARLEQUIN®
Live the emotion

HSR0507

SILHOUETTE

SPECIAL EDITION™

COMING IN JUNE

HER LAST
FIRST DATE

by *USA TODAY* bestsellling author
SUSAN MALLERY

After one too many bad dates, Crissy Phillips
finally swore off men. Recently widowed,
pediatrician Josh Daniels can't risk losing his
heart. With an intense attraction pulling them
together, will their fear keep them apart?
Or will one wild night change everything…?

**Sometimes the unexpected
is the best news of all….**

REQUEST YOUR FREE BOOKS!

2 FREE NOVELS PLUS 2 FREE GIFTS!

Passionate, Powerful, Provocative!

YES! Please send me 2 FREE Silhouette Desire® novels and my 2 FREE gifts. After receiving them, if I don't wish to receive any more books, I can return the shipping statement marked "cancel." If I don't cancel, I will receive 6 brand-new novels every month and be billed just $3.80 per book in the U.S., or $4.47 per book in Canada, plus 25¢ shipping and handling per book and applicable taxes, if any*. That's a savings of almost 15% off the cover price! I understand that accepting the 2 free books and gifts places me under no obligation to buy anything. I can always return a shipment and cancel at any time. Even if I never buy another book from Silhouette, the two free books and gifts are mine to keep forever.

225 SDN EEXJ 326 SDN EEXU

Name	(PLEASE PRINT)	
Address		Apt.
City	State/Prov.	Zip/Postal Code

Signature (if under 18, a parent or guardian must sign)

Mail to the **Silhouette Reader Service™:**
IN U.S.A.: P.O. Box 1867, Buffalo, NY 14240-1867
IN CANADA: P.O. Box 609, Fort Erie, Ontario L2A 5X3

Not valid to current Silhouette Desire subscribers.

Want to try two free books from another line?
Call 1-800-873-8635 or visit www.morefreebooks.com.

* Terms and prices subject to change without notice. NY residents add applicable sales tax. Canadian residents will be charged applicable provincial taxes and GST. This offer is limited to one order per household. All orders subject to approval. Credit or debit balances in a customer's account(s) may be offset by any other outstanding balance owed by or to the customer. Please allow 4 to 6 weeks for delivery.

Your Privacy: Silhouette is committed to protecting your privacy. Our Privacy Policy is available online at www.eHarlequin.com or upon request from the Reader Service. From time to time we make our lists of customers available to reputable firms who may have a product or service of interest to you. If you would prefer we not share your name and address, please check here. ☐

SDES07

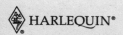

HARLEQUIN®

American ROMANCE®

**is proud to present a special treat this
Fourth of July with three stories
to kick off your summer!**

SUMMER LOVIN'
by
**Marin Thomas,
Laura Marie Altom
Ann Roth**

This year, celebrating the Fourth of July in Silver Cliff,
Colorado, is going to be special. There's an all-year
high school reunion taking place before the old
school building gets torn down. As old flames find
each other and new romances begin, this small
town is looking like the perfect place
for some summer lovin'!

*Available June 2007
wherever Harlequin books are sold.*

www.eHarlequin.com

HAR75169

COMING NEXT MONTH

#1801 FORTUNE'S FORBIDDEN WOMAN—Heidi Betts
Dakota Fortunes
Can he risk the family honor to fulfill an unrequited passion with the one woman he's forbidden to have?

#1802 SIX-MONTH MISTRESS—Katherine Garbera
The Mistresses
She was contracted to be his mistress in exchange for his help in getting her struggling business off the ground. Now he's come to collect his prize.

#1803 AN IMPROPER AFFAIR—Anna DePalo
Millionaire of the Month
This ruthless businessman is on the verge of extracting the ultimate revenge…until he falls for the woman who could jeopardize his entire plan.

#1804 THE MILLIONAIRE'S INDECENT PROPOSAL—Emilie Rose
Monte Carlo Affairs
When an attractive stranger offers her a million euros to become his mistress, will she prove his theory that everyone has a price?

#1805 BETWEEN THE CEO'S SHEETS—Charlene Sands
She'd been paid off to leave him. Now he wants revenge and will stop at nothing until he settles the score…and gets her back in his bed.

#1806 RICH MAN'S REVENGE—Tessa Radley
He'd marry his enemy's daughter and extract his long-denied revenge—but his new bride has her own plan for him.

SDCNM0507